The Bird That Nobody Sees

(FRUGALITY – Book 2)

By

Stuart Ayris

Paperback Edition

Prologue

It begins with a washing machine.

And it ends with angels.

The electrical appliance in question, the defunct washing machine that really triggered all that was to follow, was housed in a low outbuilding in the concrete beer garden of The Setting Sun Public House in Chelmsford, Essex. The building had been used by previous landlords to store all manner of pub trade remnants, from broken chairs to obsolete slot machines, cracked mirrors and old pieces of carpet. The current landlord, however, had cleared everything out except for the washing machine. He liked order. He found it healthier to work in a clean space. The washing machine wasn't plumbed in and had no discernible use. The round door was hanging on by a thread, or to be more exact, a rusty metal pin, and there were dents and scratches all over the once pristine white surface. But despite its woeful appearance, it still held pride of place in the outbuilding, kept safe from the prying eyes and scrutiny of others thanks largely to a hefty padlock and the fact that a beer garden twenty feet square and poorly paved with dirty concrete slabs is not ever going to be the province of anything other than the most loyal of patrons.

On the morning of New Year's Day, 2011, Sean Parsons, landlord of The Setting Sun, sat cross-legged on the floor staring into his washing machine. Having bemoaned the round door for its precarious bearings and life in general for being so entirely against him, he removed a small white plastic bag from the metal drum. He then pulled out the rectangular receptacle that was used to hold the powder and conditioner and retrieved two smaller bags, each as tightly packed as the first and each bound with tape. He laid the three packages before him and surveyed them as if they were his children and he was about to send them off on their first day of school.

4

It was when he was at the height of his concentration that the coarse blare of a horn blasted into Sean's morning. He crammed the three bags into the powder/conditioner drawer, not wanting to risk the greater visibility afforded by the drum and its shambles of a main door, clinging to life as it was, a port hole on a wreck just demanding a final moment of dignity. But Sean Parsons wasn't one for sentiment – or dignity for that matter. He stood up and kicked the forlorn door, not hard, but hard enough. The force of the motion led to the bent pin snapping. The washing machine door fell to the floor, performing a half-hearted pirouette before coming to rest at Sean's feet. He didn't like days at the best of times and this, clearly, was going to be another year full of days just like all the others. The horn blared again.

Sean emerged from the gloom of the outbuilding and stomped into the beer garden, all scowl and temper and simmering rage.

"Can't you just knock on the door like everyone else?"

The van driver to whom Sean had addressed this less than chirpy question grinned from the safety of his cab. He had parked down the alleyway that ran along the right-hand side of The Setting Sun and sat grinning through the closed and misted up glass. His fragrance of choice was one of cigarettes and pasties and his hair looked like it had been smoothed back from his tanned brow by a greased up garden rake. As he saw the miserable landlord approaching he wound down the window and felt the cold midday air upon his face. Thus was his pungent odour released into the fragile winter sky.

"Come on Sean mate. Cheer up! It's a new year! Now open up the old hatch and let me deliver you the finest quality spirits *your* money can buy."

Sean shook his head not in rebuttal but in contempt as the driver reversed his van. He felt it wholly immoral that fate had decreed he should depend on idiots such as this just to scratch out a living. The driver jumped out and opened up the cellar hatch in the ground. Pulling out a pallet trolley he began loading it with wooden crates from the back of the van, crates full of whisky and vodka whose labels had quite clearly been produced by some amateur computer enthusiast.

Sean looked on dispassionately. Needs must. At times like this he would keep telling himself that the pub was just a stepping stone. He had long been of the opinion that he was surely meant for bigger things than this.

"Phone's ringing, mate."

"Sorry?" replied Sean.

"Your phone. In the pub. It's ringing."

The phone was indeed ringing. Sean left the driver to his work and his sickeningly cheerful demeanour and went back in the pub via the back door, expecting news that was going to do little to elevate his mood. He guessed it would be either the hospital informing him that his mother had taken a turn for the worse, or the brewery closing him down.

The driver unloaded the last of his tax-free French Super Marché whisky and the Vodka he had bought at a knock-down price from a bloke in Tooting in late November. When he was done he slid the bolt across the top of the hatch and snapped the brass padlock shut. It was then that he noticed the door to the outbuilding was slightly ajar. He had never seen it unlocked in the two years he'd been delivering to The Setting Sun. Not only was it unlocked, but the padlock dangled from the handle with the key protruding from it. Perfect. Never one to miss out, he mulled things over. He was what would be referred to in Court as 'an opportunist'. He had a pallet trolley and a van. And there was a washing machine – a decidedly knackered looking washing machine - but years of experience had taught him that for every 'second-hand' item there's a willing buyer somewhere.

In times of austerity, such as these, even good people will justify the purchase of stolen goods. It's about how you rationalise the act, not the act itself. Everybody knows that.

An opportunist moves like a shark in the ocean. He scents his prey and the rest is history. And like Kaiser Soze – pfff – he's gone…

As the driver careered out of the alley it soon become apparent to him that although he had snapped the padlock shut on the door of the outbuilding and pocketed the keys, he hadn't secured the back door to his van. A good thief plans and takes his time. An opportunist, well, he just takes his chance. The sharp left hand turn out onto New London Road had toppled the unsecured washing machine onto its side and the first pot-hole in the road had succeeded in flinging open one of the two rear doors of the van. The driver looked fretfully into his mirror. He had a decision to make. He wasn't aware that at that stage Sean was upstairs packing a bag to drive up to Nottingham to see to the body of his deceased mother. Thus his fear of being caught was momentarily misplaced. But an opportunist doesn't acknowledge such feelings – it's all about the hush and the rush and the squeal and the appeal. No time for being organised and certainly no time for slowing down. The left hand-turn into Redmayne Drive, just a hundred yards further down the road saw to the final unveiling of that poor misused appliance.

The driver slammed on the brakes the moment his trusty van had deposited his purloined goods noisily into the road. There had not even been an umbilical cord to lend grace to the descent. Just bang and clank and clonk and silence. There it was, a few feet from a bemused Rod Langford. A stolen washing machine minus a door with fifty-four amphetamine tablets and twenty-seven ecstasy tablets in the conditioner compartment and, ironically, 137 grams of cocaine in the powder compartment.

Rod stood there, his hands in his little pockets looking about as cool as anyone could who has just had a washing machine land in front of them. The flustered driver leapt from his cab and hurtled around to the back of the van all ready to load back up his stolen goods.

"Alright?" said the driver when he saw Rod staring at the machine.

"Alright?" replied Rod.

"It's a washing machine. Fell out the back of the van."

Rod considered the validity of this statement.

"Do you want a hand getting it back in?" he asked.

"Do you want it for thirty quid?"

"Thirty quid?"

"Yeah. Thirty quid."

"It hasn't got a door."

"How much is a door going to cost you?" reasoned the driver.

"Twenty," replied Rod.

"Twenty-five."

"Ok," said Rod. Twenty-five quid for a washing machine. No more trips to the launderette in town. Liz would be over the moon.

"How am I going to get it to mine though?"

"Where do you live?"

"Just down the end there on the right. Pearce Manor."

"Give us thirty and you can take this pallet barrow. That will do you."

"What should I do with the barrow once I'm done with it?"

"Up to you. Loads more where that one came from."

Rod withdrew his wallet from the inside pocket of his leather jacket and took out thirty pounds. The satisfied driver jumped back up into his van, did a three point turn, mounted the kerb and sped away. Job done. He had made a miserable git more miserable and a little man happy. Not a bad morning's work. Rod too had reason to be pleased. Only this morning Liz had sighed at the pile of washing that needed to be sorted and taken to the launderette. The days are long gone when a man can go out and kill a bear to bring home to his cold and hungry wife but she would undoubtedly be pleased with today's capture.

But it was as Rod was wheeling his newly acquired appliance back to his flat, just a couple of hundred yards down the road, that his life changed forever. Someone who is technically classified as a midget can only reach so high it seems.

And so thought the two police officers who, in their unmarked car, rounded the corner onto Redmayne Drive some moments later, to come to the aid of a small sweaty man in a leather jacket who was struggling with a washing machine that had quite clearly, by this stage, had enough. The officers got out and watched as Rod did all he could to bump the trolley up the kerb outside his flat. Each time it thudded back down he had to brace the whole thing to stop it pushing him over into the road and landing on top of him. Looking at each other with a certain amount of disbelief at the fact Rod had not noticed their presence the officers got out of the car and approached him.

"Having a bit of trouble?" enquired the first.

Rod turned sharply, keeping hold of the trolley as he did so – perhaps the worst thing he could have done. The washing machine teetered and tottered and ever so slowly, but in a way that could not be stopped, lurched forward scraping the policeman's shins and landing on its side on his shiny black boots. The powder/conditioner dispenser popped open and deposited its goods at the feet of the other policeman. It all happened in seconds.

Doing his best not to laugh at the plight of his colleague who was now red-faced and glaring, the uninjured policeman picked up the three white bags, inspected them and grinned. And so it was that Rod Langford was arrested and charged for possession with intent to supply and, even more unfortunately, assaulting a police officer.

Chelmsford Magistrates Court is at the top of Chelmsford High Street, that steep hill lined by banks and jewellers, fashion retailers and fast food restaurants. The wide, pedestrian-only thoroughfare gives what the local council have been known to call 'a Parisian feel' to what is otherwise a non-descript stretch of characterless commercial enterprise. During the day, particularly Saturdays, people scrabble backwards and forwards, up and down in search of items and articles and remnants and goods that they believe will enhance their existence. The receipt is as important as the purchase and the credit card is the king of all kings. There's a monotone to it all, a colourless aspect that just makes you want to weep.

At night there is a hiatus as the High Street is swept clean and the revellers enter the scene. It always begins the same – foolery Tom foolery and high jinx jazz with a splattering of frolic and jollity fun. But come late eve when drink and drugs have addled the minds and frazzled the nerves, well that is when the foolish become the fractious and the inebriated become the indignant. There's a staggering and a posturing and a wailing and a flailing. Words change. Language changes. It is all of a sudden an alien persuasion that has persuaded the Chelmsford nation to recoil at beauty and retreat from all that is good. That's what the two Police vans at the bottom of the High Street are for. And that's what the Magistrates Court at the top of the High Street is for. Drink and drugs on a Saturday night are just a one-way ticket on the invisible Essex cable car that leads only to judgement.

And the best view of all this is from the steps of that sandstone building through whose doors so many have ultimately stepped.

"Mr Langford," said the frowning, coarse-haired, hard-boned magistrate. "We find you guilty of being in possession of illicit substances of a sufficient quantity that would indicate an intent to supply. Your defence that the white goods in which the drugs were concealed had 'fallen off the back of a van' does not mitigate your guilt in the proceedings. We also find you guilty of assaulting an officer of the law. Your conduct in all aspects has been most unsavoury – as has your continual denial of your obvious guilt. You are hereby sentenced to four months imprisonment. Take him down."

And take him down they did – to HMP Chelmsford. One minute you're high on the happy side thinking that you are doing a good deed for your beloved, the next you are sitting in a prison cell contemplating your fate.

It's a weird old life at times.
As you're about to find out.

1. The Mad, The Bad and The Aesthete

LOGIN - ROD
PASSWORD *******
NEW

On Friday 26th August, at 11:30 pm, I'm going to kill someone - not worked out how or who or where but if you're reading this then it wasn't you. You just got lucky I guess. Today is 26th June 2011 and I've just got out of Chelmsford prison. Put inside for something I didn't do. Just like The Shawshank Redemption but unlike that bloke in that film I did my time. Two months of a four months stretch. I didn't need no posters or chess pieces or whatever it was he used. That was just a film anyway. This is real life.

As the whole country will one day know, my name is Rod Langford. When I do what I do the papers might call me something else, give me a name. Depends how I do it. Something for me to think about. Something for me to consider. Plenty of time for thinking and considering. Funny. I've been inside for the last two months and thought about nothing but killing someone when I got out. It's only now I'm on the outside that I see I've got time to think about the details, the little things that will make it special. Prison is a hard place to look at details. But now I'm back in the world, details are everywhere. Bang - I'm going to kill someone. Bang - it's going to be beautiful.

We live in a one-bedroom flat in Chelmsford - me, the wife, the dog. Been there about a year, give or take my time inside. Changes a man, prison. It does something to you in a way not many people could deal with. You've got to be hard to survive it. You can't understand unless you've been there. If anything, I'd recommend it. Gives you time out of your life to work out what you really want to do, what you really want to achieve.

My wife is called Elizabeth, Liz. The dog is called Jasmine. It's some sort of terrier type thing, white and scraggy. Jasmine. Liz thought it was a girl at first so gave it a girl's name. When she found out it was a boy she said she couldn't change the name because it would confuse the dog. Don't get me wrong, Liz is lovely, god she is, and she definitely isn't stupid - but that dog is as bent as they come.

Liz started smoking outside when I was banged up. Makes sense I suppose. We only rent the flat and she would have been well vulnerable if the owner came round snooping when I weren't there. If he caught her smoking it would have been bad, her all defenceless and that and him some ropey old bastard who probably knocks one out over daytime soaps whenever he gets the chance. So we smoke outside now. It's only a small block anyway - nine flats on three levels. We're at the top so it's just a case of nipping downstairs. Seeing the stars does me good anyhow. Not much of a view of those from your cell window. Bars yeah, stars no.

It's so good to sleep under a duvet with Liz. She snores a bit but I don't mind that - reminds me she's there. When you're inside, night-time goes on forever. Now I'm on the out it just goes so fast. Sometimes Liz grinds her teeth which really does do my head in but then it beats laying awake on a cot waiting for the screws to bang on your door.

Three in the morning is the time where all your worries are massive and scary. I have memories you wouldn't believe. There's times I've been so close to exploding but have somehow managed to keep it all in. Three in the morning doesn't scare me no more. It's become a time for planning instead of worrying, working it all out instead of imagining it all falling apart. That's where I am now. I am capable of absolutely anything mate, absolutely anything. I know that now.

You think this world is a safe place, living in your pretty houses with your jobs and your money and your straight pets? Well it's not - not whilst I'm around.

So I lie dopey on the sofa and close my eyes with murder on my mind, a gay dog muttering in its gay sleep and Liz grinding her teeth in the other room whilst the late night cars beep their late night hooters into the Essex sky. It's a bloody symphony - a bastard prison, murderous mindfuck symphony. I don't dream. Men like me don't dream. We just crash out - then, for some reason, we're made to wake up.

And that's why it hurts.

FILE

13

SAVE AS "WIDEAWAKE"
SAVE

Chelmsford is the county town of Essex and has recently been given full 'city' status. Nobody really knows what that means except for a few local councillors whose bonus may well equal the combined annual pay of the people they have laid off throughout the year. So this new 'city' is a half hour train ride from London and in May 2011 had a population of just over 100,000. It has a cathedral, a prison, a Magistrates Court, a Crown Court, a General Hospital, two Psychiatric Hospitals, a football ground and a county cricket ground. It caters for the mad, the bad and the aesthete - any of whom can regularly be seen frequenting any of the aforementioned institutions.

From its central hub, Chelmsford sprawls through areas of semi-affluence and semi-poverty, conservative in its responses and eager to please. It certainly does not abound with wealth nor does it scrabble around on its knees. But there are the rich and there are the poor no doubt - just not in sufficient numbers to be acknowledged. People will give the Big Issue seller a five pound note and wait patiently for their change. It's that kind of town. Sorry – city.

Chelmsford is a statistician's dream – a place where the average prevails and those at either end slip slide away into the gutter or float off to the stars. Not much of note happens in Chelmsford but when it does, it's big news - only for a while though. The beat of its heart is slow and rhythmic and quick to settle when startled. It is ringed by surrounding villages which are but the cotton wool that insulates the county town from significant harm. It is a commuter's paradise (if there is such a thing) but that does not mean all is forever well within its environs.

The block where Rod lived is called Pearce Manor. It veers off to the right at the end of Redmayne Drive which is itself off New London Road - the long traffic strewn road that connects the edge of town with the centre of town. At one end is The Setting Sun Pub and at the other is Essex Cricket Ground. The Red Lion, The Orange Tree

14

and The Queen's Head are at various points in between to service the weary traveller. Equally strategically placed along New London Road are a Funeral Director's, a School, a Solicitor's office and a Bed and Breakfast.

New London Road not only connects the external to the internal but provides the essential services required for the fallen and the falling. In the months to come, Rod Langford would invariably never get further than The Setting Sun; had he availed himself, at an earlier age perhaps, of the school and perhaps a decent solicitor, this book may never have been written.

Getting to The Setting Sun, or The Sun as the regulars called it, was simple for Rod - down the stairs, do a left at the front of the block of flats, go two hundred yards, left onto Redmayne Drive then right at the junction with New London Road. Another hundred yards and there you have The Setting Sun. Were you to see an exterior photo of it, displaced and in isolation, you may think it to be rather a quaint place perhaps, a country Inn replete with a Specials Menu, wooden panelling and the best fake fireplaces your money could buy. The large bay window in the centre in between two wooden doors which are in turn flanked by sash windows and the three identical sash windows on the upper floor lend a country house feel to what is ostensibly just a place where people get drunk. Two white chimneys protrude from the grey slate roof looking down proudly upon the colourful flowers that spew from the hanging baskets nailed to the front of the pub.

But just as images can be deceiving, so certain pubs can be about more than just the alcohol. No, The Setting Sun could in no way be referred to as a chic establishment. But the people that drank there, the regulars, well, they were a different class entirely. The same could not be said however of the landlord.

When he had leased the pub a year or so earlier, Sean had put up the money jointly with a cheerful soul called Steve. After just a few weeks of the new tenancy, Steve moved back up to Middlesbrough - or so Sean had informed everyone at the time.

Rumours of a freezer full of northern lad were slow to abate and have never entirely gone away. Just pub talk though. Mostly.

As you enter the pub, the bar is directly in front of you. There is a doorway to the right that leads into the pool and darts room and the toilets where people used to do drugs. To the left as you go in is the rest of the pub, a few tables and some scattered chairs and the fire door out to the concrete beer garden; and the toilets where people still do drugs. Apparently. It is very much a pub frequented by people who just can't be bothered to go into town or to go home – and it is none the worse for it.

"Yes mate?"

"Pint of cider please," said Rod.

"Three twenty."

"Cheers."

Sean poured Rod his pint, put the money in the till and went into the kitchen behind the bar. He took two knives from a crooked drawer and began to sharpen them against one another, slowly at first and then so fast it seemed he would go on sharpening them forever. Eventually he slowed down and sat on a paint-covered stool, sweat forming on his brow like condensation on a grimy window. The knives, shiny, hard and oh so sharp, rested meekly upon his lap, tamed and glowering. It was as if he were trying to summon some sort of evil genie from them who would work at his behest.

There were two men at the bar who had paid no attention to Rod from the moment he had walked in and had long viewed Sean as no more than an accoutrement, much like the fruit machines or the payphone. They were two of the regulars and paid little heed at first to newcomers.

Although Rod lived just round the corner, it had been the first time he had been in The Setting Sun. Pubs had never really been his thing, but when you're planning a murder, scheming over a pint just seems so right.

"Check this one out, Danny mate," said the slimmer of the two men.

"Go on then," replied the other, his straggle bearded face all lager froth and glee.

The first man took a pack of cards from the back pocket of his jeans, shuffled them and spread them out along the beer-stained-fag-stained bar.

"Pick a card."

Danny duly picked a card.

"Now show it to me. Good. Six of Clubs."

"Now what?"

"Pick another card."

"Ok"

"Show it to me. Good. Three of diamonds."

"What now?"

"Pick another card."

"This is a shit trick, Ray."

"Who said it was a trick?"

"Well what are we doing then?"

"Just proving you'll do anything I tell you to do - now buy me a drink you fat bastard."

"Now you can pick these up you cheeky fuck," replied Danny, sweeping a few of the cards off the bar and onto the floor.

"Two lagers, Sean. If you can spare the time, mate."

And that's what it's like in every pub in the country, every wonderful downtrodden beautiful oasis that is so necessary amidst the arid landscape of our hectic modern days.

One of the playing cards had landed in Rod's cider. He looked into his glass, having seen the card float down like a sycamore leaf. The three of diamonds stared up at him all soggy and morose and entirely un-diamond-like.

"Now that's a fucking trick, Ray! That's a fucking trick!" declared Danny. "Three of diamonds! Would you credit it?"

Rod looked up at Danny, retrieved the sodden card and handed it back to him.

17

"Sorry mate. Just a laugh. I'll get you another pint. Cider yeah? A cider as well please Sean."

Sean poured out the drinks and Danny invited Rod to sit with him and Ray. Rod didn't like bar stools as a rule. He had never found a cool way of getting himself onto one. So he just remained where he was.

"I'll stand, it's okay."

"Yep, whatever you want. I'm Danny by the way. This is Ray."

Rod nodded his head and continued to lean against the bar.

"I'm Rod."

"Cheers Rod. Cider's for Rod, Sean."

It was three o'clock in the afternoon. The Setting Sun was notorious for opening at various times purely dependent upon the fluctuating mood of the landlord. Beams of daylight spiked in through the gaps between the blinds and lit upon the dirt and dust that gathered on the floor. Sean ambled out from behind the bar and switched on the quiz machine, the fruit machine and the jukebox – about the only three things in his life that sparked to his touch. The quiz machine flashed eagerly to life almost instantly, the fruity blinked on and off wildly before kicking into gear and the jukebox didn't respond at all. Sean took such rejections personally, adding them to the growing list of slights he seemed destined to suffer.

"Looks like Sean's got himself some new joggers, Ray."

Ray looked round and saw Sean putting some money into the fruity.

"The only thing new about those is the stains from last night when he slept in them. What's the point of wearing jogging bottoms when the only running that gets done anywhere near them is by any bird within a hundred yard radius?"

"You see them, Rod," said Danny all conspiracy and spy-like. "Don't even fit him. More crack in them joggers there than gets sold in these toilets. Keep that to yourself though, mate."

Danny winked and Rod nodded.

18

Sean then disappeared through the open doorway where the non-drug toilets and the pool table were. Before long, darts could be heard thudding into the dart-board in the corner, thudding so hard you could almost hear the pool balls quaking.

Danny and Ray drank and chatted as they supped their pints, including Rod in the conversation when they could. When it was Rod's round, Danny and Ray declined. Both were teachers and their school day off sick was almost over. They shook Rod's hand when they left saying it was good to meet him and that they hoped to see him again for that pint he owed them, expressing surprise that they had never met him before that day. And it was only when they had all gone that the dart board gained a measure of relief from its pounding. You could have almost heard it sigh.

LOGIN - ROD
*PASSWORD *******
FILE
OPEN "WIDEAWAKE"

Met my mates Danny and Ray down The Sun for an afternoon beer-up. Good blokes. Sean the landlord was miserable as usual. Could do with a new pair of joggers too. Had them ones on ever since I known him, the dirty bastard. He's got a couple of knives back in his kitchen though. Something to bear in mind maybe.

Ray did this great trick on Danny. Right laugh. They had to leave early to do a bit of marking. Wish I had teachers like them in my day. Not that I was at school much. Waste of time. There's things in this life you can't be taught in any school if you know what I mean. Never did me any harm not going. You don't get mates like I got by knowing your maths and stuff. And you don't kill by having lessons in it. It's a different way of thinking, a totally

19

different way of seeing the world. When you
know you're gonna kill, it lightens up your
whole life. There's a power in you that not one
person on this earth could stand up to.

Liz is working tonight up at Wilkos by the
Miami roundabout. Got the flat to myself. Dog
knows better than to bother me when I'm on my
own. I don't watch any crap on the telly and I
don't listen to any crap on the radio. It's
just me and my thoughts all the way.

This world ain't ever seen nothing like
me.

SAVE

But it has, Rod. It has. Every town and city and village in this
nation is teeming with the disaffected and the dissatisfied. Everywhere
there are people who have been swallowed up from birth, chewed to
pieces during adolescence and spat tumbling out onto the ground in
adulthood. And the sadness when you sit on the bus is that you look at
the schoolchildren and can almost see which of those will grow to
love and which will grow to hate. Can it really be from such an early
age that our lives are determined? Freud would have it so and perhaps
politicians too. But me? Nope. No way. A child on the bus with his
shirt hanging out and his hair a mess is just a child on the bus with his
shirt hanging out and his hair a mess. And that young girl covered in
make-up, will she find herself pregnant at fifteen and the victim of a
brief and loveless marriage? Maybe. But then she may end up being
the most beautiful woman that ever lived. People are condemned only
when we condemn them. That's all.

The world has seen plenty of horrors and there's no denying
that. And it's fair to say that it hasn't seen too much of angels. But
that doesn't mean one might not be just around the corner.

2. Dance, Dance, Wherever You May Be

It is said in some quarters that to be classified as 'suffering' from dwarfism a person must have an adult height of less than four feet ten inches. Roderick Stephen Giles Langford was four feet nine and a half inches tall, thereby meeting the classification criterion by half an inch. It did not sit well with him. It did not sit well with him at all. The fact that he did not have the condition known as disproportionate dwarfism was of little consolation. It was the very fact that he was entirely in proportion that added to his anger. Why pick on me? Look at the others – they're the ones you should be looking at – they've got massive hands and everything. I'm just short. Another half an inch and you wouldn't have a card to play. You wouldn't even notice me. Massive hands they've got and short little legs, really short. And massive hands.

So Rod Langford was forty one years old, four feet nine and a half inches tall and, as has been noted, entirely in proportion. His face ever bore an expression of one who is perpetually flinching. His brown eyes would have hidden if they could beneath his thick eyebrows but no matter how much he frowned, his eyes still had to face the scrutiny of the world. The lines of his high brow sought to distract the staring onlooker with their headlines but to no avail. Rod had a smooth face that seemed incapable of producing stubble. As such he was often mistaken for being much younger than his years. Not good when you are the average height of an eleven year old. But for one so small, he was ever so visible. The hair upon his head was dark and unruly, a little grey above the ears and a little ginger at the tips, straggly down to his neck and on past his shoulders. He almost always wore baggy jeans, a leather jacket and a variety of Led Zeppelin T-shirts. But all most people ever saw of him was his littleness.

Rod's leather jacket was his pride and joy. It had been his true outer skin for more than ten years. During that time he had covered it with badges and patches depicting his favourite bands. He had got most of them from Chelmsford Market and one or two from having gone to see the bands live. Black Sabbath, Iron Maiden, Metallica, Judas Priest, Motorhead, Slayer and Megadeath were of course all represented. And then there were Venom, Pantera, Queensryche, Dio, Celtic Frost, Sepultura and Anthrax. Not to mention Merciful Fate, Helloween, Napalm Death, Carcass and Morbid Angel. It was a fine collection of which he was rightly proud – the enamel badge of Celtic Frost and the patch of Morbid Angel being those that gave him the most pride. All his badges combined to make him feel so much bigger. With his jacket on he felt somehow that people would be drawn to inspect the badges and not notice his stature.

It could rightly be said that Rod was not disabled by his dwarfism but by society's response to it. It could equally be argued that bar stools are tricky buggers at the best of times; for they are apt to reduce the stature of any who sit upon them for an excessive amount of time - regardless of height.

"Ray, I can feel blood going round my brain," said Danny blankly, having spent the entire afternoon sitting on a barstool in The Setting Sun. "Something's happening to me."

"You're just hammered, Dan," replied Ray as his pound coin urged Joy Division into life, if life it could be called. His back was to his friend and his mind was, not the for the first time, revelling in the eighties.

"Seriously, Ray, you need to call an ambulance. I'm serious here."

Ray turned and saw the fear in his friend's eyes. Even his beard look scared.

"Sean mate. Can you phone an ambulance? Something's up with Danny."

Sean silently picked up the phone at the pool table end of the bar and did the necessary.

Ray helped Danny off the barstool and when the ambulance arrived, the stricken drinker was sitting on the floor with his legs outstretched, being propped up by the wooden base of the bar. He looked drunk. Actually he was drunk. But he was led to the ambulance all the same, convinced that his time on this earth was dwindling rapidly. For once, even Ray had to accept, Joy Division weren't really helping matters.

Whilst Danny and Ray were waiting in that godforsaken place, an elderly man walked in with a tray seemingly super-glued to his palm. He held the tray aloft as if carrying champagne flutes across a crowded room. The lines on his pale face were surely etched with charcoal and his legs were so thin it was a wonder they bore him at all. But alcohol can at times render a scene hilarious when at other times those same eyes would be overcome with a very different emotion. The giggles of the two friends from The Setting Sun did nothing to endear them to the medical profession and on this occasion it was confirmed that Danny was not in fact dying.

Elizabeth Langford had been working at Wilkos Supermarket for seven years, mainly on nights. It was one of those twenty-four hour stores and was just a few minutes walk from Pearce Manor, on the other side of the Miami Roundabout, so called because of the adjacent Miami Hotel. You could see both the hotel and the supermarket from The Setting Sun - if you happened to be in one of the upstairs rooms.

Liz had short dark hair that curled down from a centre parting and she had the face of an apple - reddened in the cheeks and almost perfectly round. She would often look on the verge of emotions whether it be tears, pain, joy or despair, without ever actually seeming capable of expressing those emotions. Perhaps her facial muscles were lacking in some way. Regardless of whether or not it was subject to a physiological deficiency, her face was often viewed as being just blank – in-between emotions, hovering on the very edges of life. She was four feet ten and a half inches tall, thereby *failing* to meet the classification criterion of dwarfism by just over half an inch. Still, if

23

you saw her, your initial reaction may have been either to bounce her off a wall or to cover her in toffee and impale her upon a stick.

When your waking night is filled with boxes and crates and packets and bottles that you struggle to afford during your waking day, it can truly hurt. Stack 'em high and stack 'em right. Break it and you pay for it. Spill it and you clean it up. Night after night after night. Liz worked hard and she worked long. She was solid and determined and absolutely intent on not letting anyone know how she really felt - not just about her job but about her life. It was her business and her business only. She saw life as a version of death. It was a thin line that wavered always, had become blurred over the years to the point where everything lacked definition. If someone ever offered to free her from this life, she would have taken their hand and danced into the valley fearing no evil.

LOGIN - ROD
PASSWORD *******
FILE
OPEN "WIDEAWAKE"
`Dance, dance wherever you may be - for I am the Lord of Death said he...`
SAVE

You see, that's how it starts - this being enamoured with death and appalled at life. It's about injustice and dishonour and hard work achieving nothing but a sweat that won't evaporate because you can't afford that gorgeous bottle of stuff you just stacked on a shelf that is patiently waiting for someone to buy it who never did a damn days work in their lives. That's where it comes from. Whether you're a few inches beneath dwarf classification or a few inches over, it's going to grind you down. Maybe you will be lucky enough to have friends that will raise you back up to where you can't be beaten; or maybe you will just embrace the vengeance that leers before you.

Whenever Liz came home from her nightshift, she would open the door to the small flat in Pearce Manor she and Rod called home and breathe for the first time since last she left it. The bathroom was directly opposite the front door, the bedroom was to the right, the lounge to the left and there was a narrow kitchen that fed off of the lounge. And that was it. From the front door you could see every room.

The computer was set up just to the right of the door on a black metal computer table. There was no room for a chair or stool of any kind. You had to stand up to use it. But given the respective heights of the two occupants this was not as much of an ordeal as perhaps it could have been.

And when Liz came in, Rod would be lying on top of the duvet, arms and legs outstretched and fully clothed. She would gently undress him until he was naked before undressing herself. She would then pull the quilt over both of them, hold him close and wish never to awake. But hours later she would invariably be awoken to the sounds of her husband calling her dog a poof. Such was the life of Elizabeth Bella Langford.

LOGIN - ROD
PASSWORD *******
FILE
OPEN "WIDEAWAKE"
When I hear Liz coming up the stairs I scramble off the sofa and clamber onto our bed. I close my eyes and just wait for her to touch me. I'm sure she mistakes my heavy breathing for deep sleep. She takes off my clothes like she's plucking petals from a flower. I know that sounds gay but that's what it's like. When she takes off my cowboy boots and tugs off my jeans, I imagine she is popping the cap off a tube of smarties, squeezing the end so it

whizzes into the air. That's the kind of half sleep half wake state I'm in when she comes home from work. And when that duvet flops down over me it is always so cold like we're in a grave together. But when she holds me I know I'm alive. She never sees the tears. I don't cry. Tears just come out. That's two different things. I've learned that over the years. I don't shiver or shake or anything. It's just sometimes tears come out.

I have a strange sleeping pattern. I doze until Liz comes in at about eight in the morning then we both sleep until about lunchtime. I say lunchtime but when we get up we both have Sugar Puffs. We take it in turns to read the back of the packet as we sit at our fold up Ikea crap table in the bay window that overlooks the car park. Not sure where the sugar puff thing came from - maybe they're always on offer. Liz fills her bowl right up to the top with milk until the poor bastards are drowning in it. I just give them a coating. Taste better that way. It's food after all, not some sort of lumpy drink. I don't tell Liz this though. When she eats she seems so content.

Sugar Puffs are done and Saturday afternoon lies ahead of us. Might go down The Sun and introduce her to the lads. Be a good start. You see at some stage I've got to be thinking of alibis. Got to plant the seeds and create an image. Rod? No way mate! He wouldn't do anything like that. Great bloke - you've got it all wrong officer. And his wife? She's lovely too.

SAVE

3. Driftwood

The Setting Sun is not the sort of pub that really attracts anything other than regulars for the majority of the time. On Friday evenings you may get some underage youngsters testing out the adult world and Sean would serve them without compunction. He squints and they look eighteen. He blinks and his conscience is clear. They drink and look twelve. And they wake up on a Saturday morning broke and sick and on the slippery slope to adulthood.

On Saturday afternoons, the husbands that have managed to extricate themselves from the town centre where their wives are cast adrift amidst the cash and the debris and the desire will plonk themselves down on a bar stool and order a quick half followed by a rushed pint, interspersed by frequent looks over their shoulder and a missed beat of the heart every time the door opens. It's never easy to enjoy a drink when you're scared of your wife. That's a well known fact. The young and the afraid come and go and the regulars are left to keep it all going. Not that Sean ever saw things that way. He was always closer to his knives than ever he was to a real life person, be they regular or irregular.

Liz and Rod left their flat and walked to The Setting Sun. Each held the hand of the other like the paper cut-out people you used to make when you were younger. Rod gripped his wife's chubby little finger between his first two fingers as their squidgy thumbs snuggled and brought their palms closer together. He always walked with her so he was closer to the road as a way of protecting her should a speeding vehicle mount the pavement. Perhaps their mighty love would light up at their conjoined touch, blaze through him and then at the raising of his right palm he would blast the offending machine into space. Boom. You're a satellite of love.

"The usual please, Sean," said Rod coolly, despite only ever having been in the pub once before. To ask for your 'usual' or, as time

27

goes on, for the barman or barmaid to be pouring your drink when they see you walk in, well, some would say that is when you know you've made it.

Sean raised his eyebrows, drew in his chin and stiffened his neck. Such tiny but decisive motions give the face no option but to express contempt. Some people are born with such a face, others grow into it. For others still it is almost an instinct like a cough or a yawn. But when you do either of these things you know it and generally, in company, you might even apologise. But not Sean Parsons. People meant nothing to him other than hassle and irritation. It was just unfortunate that the trade in which he found himself depended upon people to sustain it. Still, that fact alone did little to temper his antipathy.

"Which is?"

"Cider." Rod turned to Liz. "What do you want beauty-queen?"

"Cider, please. Pint."

"Two pints of cider. And a bag of Frazzles. Make that two bags. No, actually, make it three."

Sean served them and they picked up their respective pints and took them to a corner table. Rod went back for the Frazzles and picked up the change Sean had left on the bar. On first sight it seemed there might be a couple of pounds missing but that was fine. Not enough to make a scene about. They were the only ones on that side of the pub. The fruit machine flashed its lights and the quiz machine looked on, puzzled. The juke box was silent, perhaps considering its fate – bling blang chinkety chinkety on one side and King Smug on the other. Yet it had not a word to say unless a coin was dropped in its slot. So often neglected but with songs in there that could change your life. And either side just cheap and tawdry purveyors of dissatisfaction.

So for a monumental moment all was Saturday quiet and England cool.

"You lucky fuck!" came a voice from the pool table side. "You lucky fucking fuck!"

Rod smiled and put his pint on the table.

"It's probably the lads," he said to Liz, reaching over to put a hand on her shoulder as he sauntered by her through the doorway to the other side of the pub all ready to greet his new friends. A moment later he returned, not sauntering at all. It was lads, but none that he knew. The words "Da plane, Da plane!" hung in the air like sinister clouds

"You look tired," said Liz reaching across the table to her husband and putting a hand on top of his. He looked into her eyes.

"I'm okay, love-machine. You're the one who was working all last night. Aren't you knackered?"

"Always."

They supped their big pints and munched their big Frazzles. Rod enjoyed a packet of Frazzles almost as much as he enjoyed sugar in his hot chocolate. But they just reminded Liz of work. And work to her was drudgery extreme and perpetual reminders of what could be. And love really didn't come into it for her. It was as much a four letter word as any other four letter word. With love came emotion and emotion was really something she didn't do. Rod would call her names such as 'love-machine', 'beauty-queen', 'love-bundle', 'sex-pot' and the like but he may have just called her 'dear' for all the impact it had on her. And it must be said that such words of affection were merely well-worn adjectives on his part. They were imparted with neither spark nor dazzle. Marriage can do that to some people though. Life can do it. But more than anything else, Chelmsford can do it.

The Setting Sun on a maudlin Saturday Chelmsford afternoon can be a dreary place at times. On this particular day, like many others before it, nothing happened. Nobody burst in through the front door; nobody put any money in the meditating jukebox. Nobody played the quiz machine and the fruity looked to be fiddling with itself. Oh to keep such poor company my jukebox friend.

"What do you want to do?" asked Rod.

"I don't know. What about you?" Liz replied.

"You want to do me?"

"What?"

"What do you want to do?" asked Rod again, leaning forward, his impulsive attempt at foreplay thwarted for the moment.

"We can do whatever you want," replied Liz. "It's up to you."

A man entered the pub, ordered a half pint, drank it, looked over his shoulder, ordered a full pint and was about to take a sip when the door opened and a dishevelled woman struggling with two shopping bags stood in the doorframe. Bang! Bang! The bags dropped to the floor like discharged shotgun cartridges. The man's pint remained on the bar. He was a walking corpse and everyone knew it, fading to grey and then to translucent, the gold ring on his finger becoming tighter and tighter with every laboured breath. And he shrank and he shrank and he shrank. By the time his wife had picked up her bags again he was the size of a shot-glass. Doing perhaps the one decent thing he had done in his life Sean walked around from behind the bar, picked the little man up from the dirty floor between thumb and forefinger and dropped him into one of the carrier bags. And the woman walked out bold and merciless into the pitiless Chelmsford streets.

Time passed and people came and went - not many, but just enough to give those present the impression they weren't just brush strokes in an Edward Hopper painting. Rod and Liz were on their third pint, which they had been drinking mainly in silence. When you are just below midget height or just above midget height, what goes on around you has a huge bearing. The trick, as they had learned, was to be resigned to misfortune. Anything that happened other than that was to be considered a bonus. But misfortune is being asked for ID at the cinema or going into a shoe shop and only having children's shoes from which to choose. A bargain falling at your feet that leads to two months in prison, that's not misfortune – that's just unnecessary. As Rod and Liz were finishing up their drinks, a voice called over to them from the bar. It was Danny.

"Alright Rod, mate? Coincidence! Fancy a beer?"

Rod could not have been more proud or delighted! God, his soul was all joy and his heart danced with his soul and his mind could not comprehend. Even murder, for the moment, lay skulking in the corner. And the jukebox longed for coinage just so it could twist again like it did last summer.

"Cheers Danny. Cider would be good."

"And for the lady?"

"She'll have a cider too please mate. Pint."

"Good girl," Danny called out to Liz, who turned her head to him. Good girl. Good dog. Good riddance. She was too far away from Danny for him to notice her eyes. He just saw her mouth move a little and from a distance a sneer and a smile is so hard to tell apart – especially when you always see the good in everybody as Danny did. And there's nothing wrong with that – nothing wrong with that at all.

Sean poured six pints, staring into each as he did so as if wishing only ill-fortune on the drinker. Danny paid him with no more thought than if he had just fed his money into the fruit machine. And Sean for his part returned from the till and deposited Danny's change on the bar in an equally impassive fashion. Transaction completed Danny put the loose coins in his back pocket and headed over to where Rod and Liz sat.

"Come and join us mate. We're going to be round the other side," said Danny, a pint in each hand.

Rod looked at Liz who just looked down.

"You can," she murmured.

"Not without you," he replied. Liz looked at him without raising her head, the pupils in her eyes rising and in doing so gaining a strength that locked him in place.

"Ok. But not for long. I need to take Jasmine out."

"Good stuff," replied Rod, hearing only the words and entirely missing the expression of sadness in his wife's eyes. He thought she was giving him her 'sexy look.' You see a man is a man regardless of how tall he is.

The pool table side of The Setting Sun was a square room about twelve feet across and fifteen feet long. Opposite the doorway was the dartboard, to the right of which was a window facing out onto New London Road. The rest of the room contained the pool table. The bar extended round on the left side with room for four barstools and at the far end were a set of male and female toilets – the former drug toilets, the windows in the top of each door still boarded up from the raid of seven years ago. A set of green lights was suspended above the pool table creating an emerald glow that created a verdant haze in the centre of the room.

When Danny walked through, followed by Rod and Liz, Ray was sitting on one of the barstools talking to another man who had no hair but about the kindest face you ever saw. His name was Alex. The two men who had delivered the Fantasy Island jibes to Rod were standing over by the dartboard. They drank up and left swiftly. Ray had been subjecting them to one of his withering stares – enough to make anyone crumble. He had seen them in the pub before and had not been enamoured with them at all. He couldn't recall what it had been that had turned him against them but that didn't really matter. He was rarely wrong when it came to first impressions and rarely was his stare unsuccessful.

"Cheers, Danny," said Ray, receiving the pint his friend had bought him.

"Thanks mate," said Alex, accepting his pint also.

Ray was about five feet seven and slight of build. His short fair hair seemed to be perpetually charged with electricity as if someone had been rubbing a balloon on it for at least half his thirty six years. Blue eyes looked out sharply from his pale face and he had a neat mouth that was just the right distance between his small nose and chin. He was always smartly turned out and alert, an intelligent man held at bay by his liking for lager, fags and a bit of the other. He was cultured, spoke fluent Italian and could converse with humour, passion and depth on an incredible variety of subjects. And when he had the blues, it was the workingman's blues, not your dreary, self-obsessed wallowing. It's people like Ray that keep the rest of us going. You may not be aware, you may not even know him, but that's the truth of it.

Danny had never been seen without his dark beard. It literally enveloped his face, great black sideburns joining it to his hair which itself was black and crazy. The lager redness in his cheeks and the reflection of the pool table lights upon his spectacles were the optimism amidst the dark pessimism of the modern world. You could only tell when he smiled, which to his credit was often, by the way his brown eyes widened and his spectacles slipped a little down his nose. His belly cellar was a lager wonderland and his blood pressure was a rollercoaster ride at the best of times. He was often thought of by the others as something of a hypochondriac, but they bloody loved him. Women loved him too, but not in the way he desired. He was the sort of bloke you would want your sister to marry. Unless of course you had a sister. Ah but that's harsh. He is great!

There is no early, potted history of Alex – what school he went to, how he coped, his family, his relationships. For it does not matter. All you need to know is that he is perfect in every moment. He judges the scene and the sense and the when not to and the how. The most he will do in defiance is frown a little but this is countered by a widening of his eyes that makes you realise immediately that the lines upon his forehead are merely a concession to what society expects. Concession need not always be seen as signs of weakness. More often than not it is a demonstration of fortitude and a deep breath taken during which he who concedes grows in a fathomless fashion. It's not about turning the other cheek but about acknowledging that none of this truly exists. Alex was Japhy Ryder and Japhy Ryder was Gary Snider – a Buddha in human form, a round-faced man of peace.

Sometimes there are people that come into your life, even if they be just on the periphery, who you wonder if ever they were young. The path from baby to child through adolescent to adult is trodden by most in a way you could almost predict, even down to the years attained, the lessons learned and the final denouement. Yet there

33

are some who just appear to have understood how to be, how to really be and you just can't envisage a time when life was all confusion to them. These people are few and they are magical. And Alex was one of them.

So they were the lads, Danny, Ray and Alex. The Setting Sun regulars - the ones who kept Sean in business and the ones that kept him sharpening his knives. Little Jon was amongst their number too, but due to his shifts at the hospital his attendance was perhaps not as regular as the others. That did not however make him any less pivotal, any less wonderful. And into their midst had come Rod and Liz Langford – two people who had never known friendship of any kind except the friendship that had once, by necessity, shown to each other. They were married. That's all. It was almost as if they were two pieces of driftwood that had come together in an ocean of bewilderment, clinging to something purely because it prevented them from going under. Some would describe that as love, others convenience. Whatever way you look at it, such a relationship can be fragile indeed, susceptible to the slightest pressures. And when such pressures comes to bear there is just no telling who will come to the most harm.

4. A Sigh Is A Sigh Is A Sigh

There are angels all over this earth. There are those with wings and there are those without wings. But all are angels. Eryn Rose was an angel with wings. It's just that you couldn't see them unless you knew where to look. She wasn't an angel who would contemplate your fate, but one of those angels who would dance with you in the car park at night as the rain tumbles and the sky rumbles and the earth crumbles whilst a little rock and roll drummer bangs and crashes from the stereo, just dance and sway and sway and sway and dance and sway and sway and sway. Now that's a proper angel, hair dripping with raindrops and face all make-up streaked and clothes sodden and eyes wide and a grin so full of smile you could light up the whole damn world. Eryn Rose. Eryn Rose. I love you Eryn Rose.

Now The Setting Sun hadn't seen too many angels in its time, or devils to be honest. It is a place for the roguish, not the bad, the wanderer, not the lost, the drinker, not the drunk. That's not to say angels did not know about it, or devils. They just never went there. Not until Eryn Rose turned up one Monday evening towards the end of June 2011.

"Look at that bird," said Danny. "She's got nothing on her feet."

"Yes she has," replied Ray.

"No, she hasn't."

"Toes mate," said Ray. "She's got toes on her feet."

"Toes are part of her foot. She's got nothing on her feet."

"So Dan. If she had a foot, right, and no toes, would you still call it a foot?"

"What do you mean?"

"What I said. If she had two feet but no toes on either of them and came in here like she just did, would you still say she had nothing on her feet?"

35

"I'd probably say 'look at that bird on the floor there - she's got no toes.'"

"So, in that case then do you reckon toes and feet are separate things, sort of like fingers? If you saw someone with no fingers, would you say they had no fingers or no hand?"

"No fingers. What are you getting at?"

"So when you said that bird has nothing on her feet do you see now that she does, even if it's just toes?"

"Ray. Just get us a fucking drink."

Eryn Rose floated. Eryn Rose sauntered. Eryn Rose just appeared in front of the jukebox. Well what else would you expect of an angel?

Nobody expects Howlin' Wolf. But Howlin' Wolf is what they got. And when you hear Howlin' Wolf you wonder how you ever got by without that thunder and roar.

I'm got to change my way of livin', this life I'm livin' ain't no
good
I'm got to change my way of livin', this life I'm livin' ain't no
good
I leave home in the morning, don't come back 'til the break of
dawn

My baby said that ain't right, I'll admit that is true
My baby said that ain't right, I'll admit that is true
She said daddy, daddy, you got to change the way you do

You know I leave in the mornin', and I don't come back 'til
dawn
You know I leaves in the mornin', and I don't come back 'til
dawn
My baby looked me in the eyes, and said daddy, you got to
change your evil way

Danny closed his eyes and nodded his head in time with the blues beat blues. Ray said not a word. You don't talk when Howlin' Wolf is a-howlin'. Even Sean had the good grace to go into the kitchen. Eryn Rose just swayed in front of the jukebox lights, side to side in slow-motion motion. She tapped her dainty feet in time on the urine vomit stained carpet and her toes cleansed everything they touched. Howlin' Wolf, a barefoot angel and two decent blokes. Now that is one decent pub. Sean never saw it though. He was out back snapping the ring pull off a tin of tuna and scowling at the still secure lid.

De ne ne ne ne ne-nar, ne ne naar….

Blues feels holes in lives.

Then Blues fills holes in lives.

Blues put on a jukebox by a beautiful barefoot swaying angel on a desolate Monday evening in a more or less deserted pub in Chelmsford, Essex, well that is just undeniable in its magnificence…

De ne ne ne ne ne-nar, ne ne naar…

"Top song, Ray."

"Yep."

"Pint?"

"Coke."

"Coke?"

"Fuck off. Lager."

"Two lagers Sean."

Poured in silence.

Scorned in silence.

Drunk in silence.

'Til almost the end.

"Any requests boys?"

It was Eryn Rose, about turned and facing Ray and Danny who sat on their stools at the bar, thinking their own thoughts and considering the fate of their own mixed-up mixed upness in peace as

37

mates do and in melancholic broken reference to tunes long past as men do.

"Any requests?"

Ray's first thought was 'take your bra off' and Danny's first thought was 'will you marry me?' As it happened, Ray requested Joy Division and Danny another pint of lager. Great, great lads.

And Eryn Rose, well she just put on a Jimmy Reed song and swayed some more.

> *They may kill me baby, bury me like they do*
> *My body might lie but my spirit gonna rise*
> *And come home to you*

> *Ain't that lovin' ya baby?*
> *Ain't that lovin' ya babe?*
> *Ain't that lovin' ya baby?*
> *But you don't even know my name*

"So what's your name, love?" asked Ray.

"Danny. Queer."

"Not you. *You* love, what's your name?"

"Eryn Rose."

"Eryn Rose," said Ray as if the words upon his lips tasted of sweet soul music.

"Eryn Rose," said Danny as if the words upon his lips tasted of lager – which they did.

"Yes, Eryn Rose. I'm an angel."

"You are love," replied Ray. "You are. Do you want a drink?"

Eryn Rose closed her big eyes. Then she opened them and smiled.

"A pint of cider please," she whispered, leaning forward, tottering on her toes.

And everybody's heart beat loudly and everybody breathed deeply and everybody smiled the smile of a child in wonder. A sigh is a sigh is a sigh. And a cider is a cider is a cider even if it's poured by a miserable old bastard in the presence of an angel.

Eryn Rose sat on a barstool between Ray and Danny swinging her legs in swaying time with the Mamas and the Papas, slow and slow and slow.

"So are you from round here then?" asked Ray.

"You've been to my flat enough times, you bender," replied Danny.

"Not you. *You* love."

Eryn Rose smiled. She liked Danny. And she liked Ray. In truth, she loved everyone. She loved you and she loved me. It's just I guess by the time we look up from our pints, Howlin' Wolf, Jimmy Reed and Eryn Rose have left the building. Sometimes, no matter how big and bold the stars, all we see is the blackness of the sky. Perhaps that's all that makes sense. Maybe it's drink and maybe it's just meant to be. Stars big and bold are hard to miss though if you really have a mind for them. And angels, well, they shouldn't have to dance barefoot in front of you before you notice them now should they?

I woke up this morning, de ne ne ne nar…

"So, Eryn Rose," continued Ray. "Are you from round this way? Just haven't seen you round here before. Don't blame you though. Dirty place. Don't get many birds in here to be honest. Not that I'm calling you a bird - you're a woman, lady, you know. Whatever you prefer."

"I'm an angel," replied Eryn Rose.

"Right." replied Ray.

Danny burped.

Ray grinned.

And Eryn Rose noticed Sean breathing deeply by the sink out back. She shuddered; then remembered she was here for a reason. And it really wasn't to drink with a pair of strangers, lovely as they were. For it was another, slightly shorter stranger, that she sought.

Rod didn't go out that Monday night. He had missed Eryn Rose and she had missed him. He had been working on his plans to kill, entirely uninterrupted by angels and the like. Although 'working' is something of an exaggeration. He was actually lying on the sofa staring at the magnolia ceiling. Liz had left for her night shift and he was in the flat just with Jasmine, the dog for whom he had scant affection. As he gazed upwards he began to see not the colour of the ceiling but small imperfections, a crack here, a mark there. The more he looked the more the smoothness dissipated. It was as if, since he had come out of prison, the world was offering up to him its stale odours, its deceptions and its dank alleyways. These things had always been there but he felt more of an affinity to them now.

The following morning Rod awoke to an empty bed. Liz was still at work. It was about five o'clock and though the sky was light, Rod's mind was dark with deep, deep, breakings. He was a small man, Rod, classified as a midget by any who care for such classification - yet his aching and his bitterness and his need were huge indeed; as large as the other side of the bed where Liz should have been. It was a white sheet, a pure and unruffled white sheet.

Rod never moved when he slept. He just kind of shut down - so when he awoke, the empty half of the bed was as pristine and perfect as a hotel bed, just without the light touch of the tearful maid. And it would hammer home to him that his love was not a love perfect or a love fulfilled or a love adorned. He loved Liz no doubt, or so he had once believed. But where was she now when he wanted to reach over with his short little arm and rub her shoulder and maybe even, if he really tried, reach her hair? I'll tell you where she was. She was at Wilkos wondering if there was any way to inject poison into the piccalilli without removing the lid. That's the truth of it.

And until I fully explore the ingredients of piccalilli I will always believe it to have been tampered with in some way or another. It just doesn't seem right - not right at all.

So it's a wonderful world of gherkins and sauces and mustards and mayonnaise. Soft and flavour and spiky and savour. God we sup and we slurp and we wave up the micros with our pots and our pans and our invisible film. And behind all the scenes of kings and queens is a woman just above midget height trying to work out a way of killing us all without being caught. All the while, her husband, just below midget height, and therefore most definitely a midget, has an angel as yet unknown to him, tickling the very edges of his wildest and wickedest dreams.

5. Giggle And Squeak

Eryn Rose was never born and she will never die. She is an angel, an idea, a thought, a spasm, a lightening, a moment. She bursts and she shimmers and she retires and she wavers. An angel is an angel only. The sands shift. Volcanoes rumble. Even the seas sigh. Eryn Rose is the mellow in the honey, the cool in the deep hot blue, the breaking of the wave and the shimmering soft of high, high comfort. She is the sparkle and the glint; the hint of a hint of a hint. She is rapture and she is fantastical. Where others wander, she soars and where you dream she inspires and cracks and breaks into a million different suns that will just shower and float into the ether of all your wondabulous thinkings. And can she fly? Of course she can fly. She is an angel.

But even angels ache.

Eryn Rose lived in a single room in a house with an angel of fine-repute and an angel undergoing his probationary period. The angel of fine repute would leave post-it notes on the communal fridge, written in red ink, usually offering some form of advice such as why Ketchup should be in the cupboard and not the fridge and what deathly properties permeated pineapple chunks that are left in opened tins. The angel in training would leave post-it notes written in green ink often contradicting the advice of the red ink person with such thoughtful remarks as "ketchup is as ketchup does" or "so?" On being presented with such erudition when reaching for her morning milk, Eryn would smile to herself and maybe even giggle a little. People were great as far as she was concerned. And angels? Well they were the best.

Angels shouldn't upset one another though. That's one of the rules.

It's strange to think that angels have rules. Surely being an angel means you are inherently good, therefore no rules are required?

Well, no. Even fine people, and angels in particular, require rules to ensure temptation does not interfere with their sole purpose – to transform lives. Regardless of height.

The Probation Office in Chelmsford is situated on the third floor of a four storey building. The building itself is on one side of a set of apartments. On the other side of the apartments is a fitness centre. It is as if those living in those oh so plush apartments have a choice the moment they set foot out of their foyer door - to do good go to the right, to get caught doing bad, go to the left. But the people in those apartments were utterly unaware that such a choice even existed. For they had money. They had jobs. They had confidence and they had ambition. And as far as they were concerned right and wrong didn't come into it any more than right and left did. Money was made. Money was spent. Money was saved. It was a wonderful life indeed. But if such an occasion arose when bad had to be done, toes had to be trodden upon and conscience had to be quelled, well no problem. That was capitalism. That was the way of the world. That was street-wise and that was a card well played.

Rod had always taken the lift up to Probation but on this, his final visit, he decided to take the stairs. He wanted to make it hurt as much as he could. Each step he took, he tensed the muscles in his thigh so his knee in turn felt a sharp pain. And as his ankle took the weight, he lifted his other foot only to repeat the process. Up and up and hurt and hurt. When you're a midget, each step is a hard one and a big one. On this day, the last visit to probation, Rod wanted to make a point to himself. You don't break me with stairs. It's not me that's disabled. I am hard and I am big. And next time, I won't get caught.

"Hi!!!"

Rod looked up at the reception desk. It was Evangeline. She was a doll turned human, make-up on legs, a balloon within a balloon and a puff of wind away from thin air. She shone like a Christmas light and Rod hated her. He wanted to rape her. He wanted to burst her. He wanted to kill her. But she wouldn't be the one. Too easy mate. Too easy.

"I'm here to see Maggie," he said in as surly a fashion as he could muster.

"How are you Roddy Roddy?" asked Evangeline, entirely ignoring what he had just said. "I know I shouldn't say this, but you are SO cute! Come on, give me a smile! You know you want to!"

Despite every conscious effort, the corners of Rod's taut lips turned upwards a little. It was sufficient to turn Evangeline into a gooey mess, giggling and squeaking. It was all Rod could hear as he sat on a ragged chair in the waiting area. Giggle and squeak. Fuckle and fuck. Take me away from all this. Please.

Ten minutes later, Maggie appeared and led Rod into the usual room. There ware a few hard-backed chairs scattered around in a half-hearted semi-circle. One of the chairs was on its back on the floor, its four legs pointing towards the window.

"The anger management lot," said Maggie, righting the chair and sighing. "Sit down, Rod. Good to see you."

Maggie had short dark hair, and a face that on a man would be handsome but on a woman seemed to lack femininity. She wore shapeless beige trousers, a white blouse and no jewellery. She had a thin mouth and a sharp nose yet her eyes counterbalanced all this anonymity with a depth that was simply breath-taking. When you have integrity, as Maggie did, you don't need lipstick or bangles to be noticed. Neither do you need to be loud and abrasive. And it is a truth that needs to be told that you don't need to be an angel to make a difference.

Rod sat on the chair that had maybe half an hour ago been thrown to the floor. Maggie did not fail to notice his choice. She was very good. And Rod didn't want to kill her. That was a bonus of which she was almost entirely unaware.

"So Rod. Last day today. This is where we're supposed to look back over the last two months, or four if you include the prison time, and see what you have learned. So where should we start?"

44

"Wherever you want. I just want to get this over with."

"Do you want a coffee?"

"Sure."

"Sugar?"

"Three please."

"Three?"

Rod nodded. Three sugars.

Maggie picked up the phone on the table beside her and ordered the coffees for herself and Rod. Moments later, a quivering Evangeline brought them in. She waggled a wiggle finger at Rod on the way out and beamed at him as if imploring him to stop being SO cute.

"Has it all been a waste of time then Rod? All this?" asked Maggie. "Just a case of turning up and listening to me talk rubbish?"

"You've been alright. It's nothing personal. Just want to get back on the straight and narrow. I've done my time. I've paid my debt. I don't know what more you people want from me."

"I know it hasn't been easy for you, but you must have learned something. Or should I say I need to report that you've learned something. Forms to be filled in. You know how it is. I don't like it any more than you do."

"Not easy? I did my bird like I was standing on my head. Like I said. I've paid my debt."

"Ok Rod. Just help me out here. Can I just at least be assured that you won't be assaulting any more police officers with kitchen appliances or dealing any more drugs? For a while at least. Once bitten, twice shy and all that."

"I was fitted up. I told you that all along. The bastard copper knew it was an accident and I'd never seen those drugs before in my life."

"It's not about whether I believe you or not. That doesn't come into it. Not in the report I have to do anyway. What you tell me is up to you. I personally think you got a rough ride. I've seen people do more who got less, if you know what I mean. For what it's worth I think you're a decent bloke who just got unlucky. Just give me some indication that you will be a little less unlucky in the future."

"Yes miss. Of course miss. Three bags full miss. Good enough?"

Rod leaned back on his chair and, ever so slowly, it toppled over and he went with it. There was nothing Maggie could do but try and keep from laughing. When Rod stood up again, he kicked the chair across the room. It hit the table leg, causing the plastic cup containing his coffee to shudder. Doing his best not to express the pain he felt in his foot he stood up to as full a height as he could muster.

"I'm done with this," he said. "Done with all of it. All of you."

Maggie, trying so hard not to smirk, just nodded and in doing so granted him permission to leave.

Rod left the room, got the money back for his bus fare, ignored Evangeline's wave and took the lift, eschewing the stairs. He'd proved his point with them on the way up. And, anyway, his left foot throbbed like a cartoon thumb. The lift seemed bigger than he had remembered. Perhaps it was just that he'd not been alone in it before. Or perhaps it's just that everything in this world grows and shrinks depending upon how you feel about yourself at any given moment.

So Probation was done. Society had punished the guilty and the guilty had bowed to its inglorious majesty. Reports completed, boxes ticked, forms signed, bus fares reimbursed and the western world rolls on, perpetuating the myth that deprivation, segregation and humiliation are required for a man to know he has done wrong. But you take a man's dignity and you just leave a gap that will be filled with the oozing oil of bitterness. You take a man's belief in fairness and you leave him with scant regard for decency. But you forgive him and you give him something far more precious - you give him something to lose.

Rod Langford was a free man again. Free to go. Free to kill. Free to let that bitter oil spread onto the diminishing pool of his conscience. The bus fare in his pocket jangled and his back throbbed from where he had fallen off the chair. You may say he didn't have far to fall. But a man who despises his life as Rod Langford did right then as he walked past the fitness centre, well that man has nowhere to fall at all. And having nowhere to fall is truly what makes a man dangerous.

LOGIN - ROD
PASSWORD *******
FILE
OPEN "WIDEAWAKE"

It's getting clearer now. I can see it or at least I can see how it will feel. On the way home from probation I saw this fox in the road. It was dead. Proper dead. There was blood and there were ants all over the fur and no way that fox could even scratch himself he was that dead. Must have been hit by a car. And you know what I thought, the first thing that came into my head? It was me that should have been driving that car that hit it. I would have loved it. Bang, squelch, screech, thud - all those great sounds. And I would have got out of the car and kicked that fox a bit, made sure he knew it was me that did it, make sure he would remember me. I was thinking like that all the way back here. I've got it in me you see, got it in me to kill. And then I thought, no, I should have been the actual car and then, no, the bumper.

Those tossers at that gym, the way they look at me when I walk by the window when they're on their bikes or the running machines or whatever they are - it's like I'm nothing, an animal or something, a fox going through their bin. Some sort of rat. That's how they look at me. Might just make one of them famous. Not that they would know it.

Must sort myself out a victim soon. Time is going to fly once I get going, once my plan starts getting put into action. Whoever it is won't know what's hit them. There will be ants and there will be blood and there'll be plenty of kicking.

Adidas fuckers!

SAVE

Eryn Rose was waiting for Rod when he came out of the Probation Office. She had been sitting behind a large shrub, humming a tune to herself. It only consisted of four or five notes but she enjoyed it so much it had made her smile. Angels, as we all know, have the ability to both smile and hum simultaneously. Actually, Angels can smile and do anything simultaneously - a marvellous attribute whose worth should never be overlooked. But what Eryn Rose did overlook was Rod. He was some hundred yards down the road when she first noticed him. She made her way out of the shrubbery and padded lightly after her small quarry. The pavement sighed as her bare feet touched it and age old cracks smoothed over at her passing. Dust settled in her wake and even the stern, humourless kerb relented a little.

Rod was entirely oblivious of the fact that he was being followed. His peculiar lack of height had always attracted the gaze of others throughout his life – well-meaning folk and otherwise. People are sometimes just curious and can't help but stare. Rod had long since given up looking about him when he walked. His eyes were ever fixed forward and downwards. The road didn't stare back. He had learned that and learned it well. Always better to see a dead animal in front of you than a live one behind you.

And of course that morning he had seen a dead animal - a fox crawling with ants. What he hadn't seen though was Eryn Rose pick the fox up, cradle it in her arms and lay it down on the neatly manicured grass verge by the Catholic Church in New London Road. The fox blood lingered upon her forearms and stained her white t-shirt - never a good choice of attire when you are picking up a dead fox but angels are partial to wearing white it must be said. And the ants? Well Eryn Rose said farewell to every single one of them and forgave them all as she did so, although fully aware that she would be more than likely to see them again were similar circumstances to arise. Short memories, ants – and barely a conscience between them.

Eryn Rose turned right onto Redmayne Drive and right again onto Pearce Manor. There was a small park in front of her and flats to her left and her right. She hadn't seen which way Rod had gone and so stood there a moment, musing. She then skipped over to the park and found herself a swing. She pushed herself off gently with the tippy tip of her toes and wafted into the air before swooning back down again, waft and swoon, waft and swoon. The blocks of flats either side leaned and fell to her waft and swoon. It was a beautiful day.

But beauty was not exactly what Liz Langford had on her mind as she trudged along Redmayne Drive on her way home. It had not been a particularly bad day. It had just been a day. And that was bad enough. She had been on an early shift at the supermarket and had just finished her thirty fifth hour of the week. The worst thing about early shifts for Liz was that she had the rest of the day ahead of her. Nights suited her fine. Nights were dark and long. It was dark when she went to work and, usually, depending on the time of year, it was dark when she got home. Black was the only colour that made sense to her, the only colour that didn't lie to her. And in the darkness, nobody could really see what you were up to.

All Liz needed to brighten her mood was to see some stupid woman on a swing at the end of her road. She let herself into the foyer door and climbed the stairs wearily to where she knew her Rod was

49

waiting. And when she opened the door to the flat he shut down the computer like he always did. Liz had noticed that and made a mental note to herself to find out what he was hiding in there. For when you live in blackness, the gloom itself really does sharpen your eyes.

When Eryn Rose felt the glare of Liz Langford's stare, she allowed the swing to slowly come to rest. And a shudder shook the joy from her for a moment. As those who dwell in darkness abhor light, so are those who live in the brightness of our days wary of darkness. Getting to Rod, and doing what she had been assigned to do, would clearly not be as easy as Eryn Rose had been led to believe.

6. Shadows Fall Just Where They Ought

"So how about it Sean?"

"How about what?"

"Getting up a pool team. Me and Danny are up for it. Right Dan?"

Danny nodded in Ray's direction.

Ray, having made his pitch, rolled up a roll-up and went out the back to smoke it. He and Danny were the only two customers in The Setting Sun on this Friday afternoon. Rod hadn't been in for the past couple of weeks, not since his probation had finished. Other regulars would come and go but none was as regular as Ray and Danny. Alex went to the pub only occasionally. He drank a little less than his friends but didn't feel quite the need to meet up so regularly. And Little Jon had ever been a slave to the vagaries of shift-work, often not knowing what he was doing from one day to the next, be it in terms of his shift pattern or his life in general.

So the sun peeked through the cracks of the Chelmsford skyline into the concrete beer garden of The Setting Sun. Thin shadows struck out across the un-swept courtyard, the yellowing leaves of untended plants casting more magical shapes on the ground than they could possibly aspire to in reality, their cracked plastic pots having forsaken them long ago. Ray gazed down at the shadows as he smoked, pausing only occasionally to look up at the sky. Without the sun there would be no shadow, he thought, wondering at the majesty of something so bright and so far away creating something so dark and so close. He finished his roll-up and returned to his accustomed place at the bar.

"And who would be in this team? Apart from you two," Sean mumbled as Ray resumed his seat.

"I don't know. This place is never exactly overrun with punters is it? Alex said he would. You need a minimum of six I think.

Little Jon would be up for it. And Derek might even give it a go. If we can just get enough to start then others will join, I'm telling you."

"Chalk it and they will come," said Danny. "Baize of dreams," he added, very pleased with himself. Sean looked at him as if he had never seen him before in his life.

"And what about you Sean? Be good for the pub, landlord getting involved."

Sean looked at Ray in much the same way as he had just looked at Danny before leaving them to serve Derek who had just walked in, right on five o'clock as usual. It wasn't that Derek worked during the day. It was just that five o'clock was the time he went to the pub. Well, we've all got to have our routines.

"Who was that bird that was in here the other week, Sean?" asked Danny, once Derek was safely nose deep in his beer.

"Which one?"

"You know - the only bird that's been in here this side of the Second World War. Kind of fit but kind of weird. She played a couple of tunes on the machine, downed a pint, had a bit of a dance to herself and left."

Sean shook his head. "No idea what you're talking about."

"She put the blues music on. Good taste that bird," added Ray.

"Do you two want another drink?" asked Sean. He generally ignored anything that wasn't going to make him money. And he was never going to make an exception for anybody.

"Two more of the same," Danny replied. "I'd have done her," he said, turning to Ray.

"Really, Dan? Do you think she would've just stood there and let you do her?"

"Not like that. I was just saying that she was alright, that's all."

"Yeah, true. Sort that sticks in the memory. Anyway - game of pool?"

Ray and Danny went through to the pool table side and put their pints on the bar. It was like having their very own perfect lounge, except they had to pay for the drinks and the pool and had to put up

52

with Sean staring at them whenever they bent down to play their respective shots. They could feel his gaze just at the edge of their hazy green baize vision; unnerving, unsettling and unspoken.

"You want a game, Sean?" one or the other would always ask eventually, knowing that the answer would always be the same.

"No. You carry on. I've got a pub to run, in case you hadn't noticed."

Ray won the first two games and Danny pulled one back before Ray won a further two.

"4-1 Danny, mate. One more before Alex gets here?"

Danny shook his head. "Nah. Get us a lager though. I'm going for a piss."

Despite having a pub to run, Sean had remained behind the bar watching Ray and Danny play their games of pool, staring at them in much the same way that Ray had stared at the shadows on the concrete. Perhaps that is what people were to Sean – just forms that struck out before him blocking out any brightness he may deign to attain.

"So Sean. This pool team idea. What do you reckon?" asked Ray, determined not to let it drop.

"You're going to have to leave it with me."

"What do you mean? Just a case of saying 'yes', surely? League is every Monday evening, you get other teams come here and they'll bloody double your takings for a start. Then there's word of mouth, you know, they'll go back to their own boozer and say how great it is here and before you know it you'll be able retire to, I don't know, Bournemouth or somewhere."

"And what about the away games?" Sean replied. "This place will be empty. And what if people come here and they hate it and then they go back to their own pub and every other pub they go to and tell people how much they hate *this* pub. Then everyone will hate it. And before you know it I'll be unemployed and living in a Bed and Breakfast in, I don't know, Bournemouth or somewhere."

"Oh, Sean, come on. Where's your spirit mate? Imagine it - The Setting Sun Pool Team - top of the league - you get a trophy for over there by the optics and loads more to come."

Sean stopped wiping up the dregs with his Carlsberg rag and looked up at Ray for the first time in the conversation. This time, when he spoke, it was as if he were hammering the words into a board with a mallet.

"Where's my spirit? Well you know what, I think it may have been in that fucking washing machine that some bastard nicked whilst I was up Nottingham a few months back visiting my dead mother. I've still got the door to the washing machine back there. If I ever find out who's got the rest of it I'll fucking kill 'em." And at that, Sean began wiping the bar again. "So that's where my spirit is," he added, addressing the soggy rag in his hand.

Danny returned from the non-drugs bathroom (he refused to use the other one in case an ex-pupil wandered in), wiping his hands on his jeans.

"What's going on then lads? You playing, Sean?"

Sean looked right through him and went back out to the kitchen area to look for something to sharpen.

"Did you know his mum had died, Dan?"

"Nope. Probably fucking topped herself."

"Ah come on mate. Bit harsh. And did you know he had his washing machine nicked?"

"Really? Who'd nick a washing machine? Actually, *how* do you nick a washing machine?"

"And it didn't even have a fucking door on it," said Ray, racking the balls up for another frame. "Your break, mate."

Danny looked quizzically at Ray before smashing the balls to all corners. The cue ball bounced off the table, clonked on the floor and rolled towards the doorway to the main bar.

Rod Langford picked it up and smiled, holding it aloft as if it were a trophy.

Eryn Rose now at least knew roughly where Rod Langford lived - the block, anyway, if not the actual flat number. And she knew the pub he drank in; if not the actual days he went there. So it would only be a matter of time before she caught up with him. But time, however slowly, was ticking. And from what she knew there was much to be accomplished if all was to turn out for the best. As you can imagine, angels very much like things to turn out for the best.

'Please take time once in a while to replenish the ice-cube tray' read the newest post-it note on the fridge.

'Please take time once in a while to leave me alone," was the reply.

"Those two," thought Eryn Rose to herself. She was of the view that an angel in training should really demonstrate a little more respect for his fully fledged angel counterpart.

It was her turn to arrange the monthly meeting anyway so she went to the sweet shop and bought four tubes of Smarties. When she returned, she spent a joyful half hour arranging the smarties on the kitchen worktop to spell out her message to her two colleagues:

Meeting 7 pm Trinity Park

Chelmsford has fifteen parks within its Borough boundary. Trinity Park is fairly typical of the majority of them. It spans twelve acres and is home to a football pitch, a cricket pitch, tennis courts and a children's play area. It has the distinction of being home to Trinity House to which the Chelmsford Museum was relocated in 1930. The Museum was founded in 1835 by the Chelmsford Philosophical Society and had been something of an itinerant institution, having spent time in Chelmsford Gaol, before finally coming to rest in Trinity House. And just inside the gates of the park is a 36 pounder Russian gun that was captured during the Crimean War. Make of that what you will.

Eryn Rose and her two colleagues rested their backs against an old oak tree and stretched their respective legs out before them. She faced north, Brando to the one side of her faced east and Renbourne to the other side faced west. Angels find the company of other angels difficult to tolerate at times as there is rarely anything about an angel that needs saving – so they try at all times to avoid eye-contact unless absolutely necessary. It even says it in the rules.

"So," began Eryn Rose, looking ahead of her as she spoke, "What's up and what's down?"

Brando was the first to speak. Again, he looked ahead only. He faced the car park that still had some cars in it, despite the lateness of the day.

"Well it seems I've been pulled off my first assignment, my first proper one, which means I guess I'm still *in training* which is, well, to be expected. It seems some people just have no faith in me."

"What assignment were you pulled from, Brando? Has it been covered or deleted?"

"Some nurse in Tollesbury – village near Maldon. Pretty screwed up by all accounts. He's been getting drunk every night in the local pub and keeps breaking into some lock-up thing they've got there in the village square."

"That nurse will be fine," cut in Renbourne casually, staring at the hedgerow in front of him. "He's been drunk for years. His wife, Penny, can handle things for now."

Brando yawned, loud enough for both Eryn Rose and Renbourne to hear. Eryn Rose smiled, of course unseen by the other two. Brando had only been on angel training for a few months and was eager to acquire the knowledge possessed by his mentor, Renbourne. But angels have time to acquire such things. In fact, they have all the time in the world.

"And how are things with your man, Eryn Rose?" Renbourne enquired.

"Slowly but surely. Although I do have a feeling it's going to be a lot more difficult than I first imagined. It's just a feeling at the moment."

"Your intuition has always served you well in the past. You should trust it. I'm going to ask Brando to work with you on this one."

"Oh I see. So I need a chaperone now, is that it?" interjected Brando. "Fantastic! I've already deserved to earn my wings yet now I need Eryn Rose to hold my hand."

Eryn Rose reached over with her right hand and put it on top of Brando's left hand. He had been digging in the dirt with his fingers and had disturbed a worm that was trying hard to wiggle away to a calmer place. Having stayed Brando's hand, she blew a kiss to the wiggly worm who winked back at her with his wiggly eye before going on his wiggly way.

"Come on, Brando. It'll be fun!"

"Yeah, yeah."

"One thing though. Both of you. No more post-it notes. They look very untidy. And what would any of the angels from the other organisations think if they saw them?"

"No more post-it notes," Brando conceded.

Renbourne nodded, unseen by Brando, but noticed by Eryn Rose.

"Goody good," she said.

A couple in love walked by, hand in hand. A young woman sat on the grass nearby entranced by her mobile phone. And over in the children's play area some teenage boys were playing on the slide doing their best to look cool whilst still clinging grimly to what remained of their childhood. It's okay lads. The practice of running up a slide will never lose either its allure or its inherent coolness. Trust me. It just hurts your knees that bit more when you get a little older. And one day your wife may stand on the periphery with your dog, woman and canine shaking their heads in unison, as your middle-aged self clambers against gravity and slip-slidiness with such courage and joy. But pay them no mind. Secretly the mere act of running up a slide only makes her fancy you all the more. And your dog? Well as soon as he sees a squirrel he will view you not as a fool but as a role model. Again – trust me. I have the grazes and the aching, forty-two year old knees to prove it.

"Well thank you for calling this meeting, Eryn Rose," said Renbourne. "I believe we have come to a decision. You and Brando will work together on this case."

Eryn Rose stood up and pulled Brando to his feet.

"Come on Brando – we've got a date with a little man!"

Renbourne watched Eryn Rose and Brando disappear across the park as they headed in the direction of The Setting Sun. He adored the enthusiasm that flowed from Eryn Rose and he hoped that Brando would come good in the end. Although the two of them had so much in common, being an angel just seemed to come that bit more naturally to Eryn Rose. Where she was prone to enchantment, Brando seemed ever on the verge of being disenchanted, as if expecting disappointment. It was almost as if situations that confirmed his pessimism were in some way more fulfilling for him purely by dint of the fact that he could at least feel himself proved right – even if he had played the pivotal role in ensuring the failure itself.

But now, alone beneath the tree in the desolation of Trinity Park, the slide unmolested and the lovers gone and the girl with the mobile phone in tears somewhere near the stark Russian Cannon, Renbourne felt a chill that was precipitated less by the setting of the evening sun than by an instinct that had long served him well. There was a darkness around Rod Langford that worried even an angel of Renbourne's experience. And he knew better than most that shadows fall just where they ought.

7. Pillowcreased Morningcheek

Night Replenishment - Customer Assistant

When the rest of the country is safely tucked up under a warm duvet, our night replenishment teams are working away to make sure customers get exactly what they want. Or to put it another way: you play a big part in delivering 'Every Little Thing Makes A Difference'.

And being Wilkos, that means much more than keeping the shelves full. You'll get involved in lots of different areas, from stock rotation to working on the tills. Just the same as customer assistants on day replenishment, you will support our warehouse staff with deliveries, ensure our aisles are tidy and clear and be supportive of other colleagues to deliver an excellent customer shopping trip at all times.

So you'll definitely need a can-do attitude and bags of initiative and enthusiasm.

It had been eight years ago when Liz Langford had seen the advert in the local paper. She had sighed and applied. When she got the job she had sighed again. And it had been seven years ago, in the early hours of a Thursday morning, when she had picked Rod up from the floor in the dairy products aisle. The first she had known he was there was when her giggling colleague had tapped her on the shoulder. Liz had turned to see a little hairy man flat on his back in a puddle of milk. She had gently put down the loaf of wholemeal bread she was about to stack and walked over to where Rod was clambering back to his feet.

"Are you okay?" she had asked. "Are you alright?"

"It's not your fault. I don't think anybody saw anyway."

"No use in crying over spilt milk, eh?" said Liz, unblinking.

"I'm not crying though am I?"

"That's true."

59

Love senses moments and it moves and it grooves, floating down from the highest of our heavens. It wades through dark waters and it bursts into the clearings of our most lingering longings. Love steps through the fields of our sighs and it brings warmth to the cold shudder of our shudderings. It dances and it skips and it rocks and it rolls. And when it sees a little hairy man floundering in a puddle of milk and a Night Replenishment Customer Assistant helping him to his feet, well…BEHOLD LOVE - FOR LOVE IS IN THE HOUSE!

And when love is in the house, even though that house be a Chelmsford Supermarket and not a church in Alabama, well the only appropriate response is Ray Charles declaring that he can't stop loving you and Diana Ross promising that mm-m-m some day, some sweet day we'll be together. Cymbals don't crash and lights don't shine and choirs rarely appear impromptu on such occasions. You just have to rely on good fortune and the beating of hearts.

Love is tender and love is a many splendored thing. Love hurts, love wounds and love scars. There's love cats and there's crazy little things called love. But most of all, there is an emotion, a sensation that nobody has ever been able to describe that totally embodies the THRILL of it all. And long may that be so.

I'm holding a loaf of bread. And I am in love.

I'm sitting in a pool of milk. And I am in love.

It's not chemicals or sonnets or any of that artifice. It is unfathomable. There's no starting it and no stopping it. You have no control over love – it is a vapour, a waft; just air at best. If mere written words could do love justice then Ray Charles would not bring me to tears. If love was but beauty acknowledged then your pillowcreased morningcheek would not make my smiles so sweet. And if love was nothing but a myth my love for you would surely not be so tangible.

I can't stop loving you. I've made up mind.

I've made up my mind.

So from sitting in a pool of milk just a few years ago, Rod was now holding aloft a white pool ball, the cue ball itself no less, and presenting it to his new friends. Progress in life can be assessed in many ways and surely such a transition as had thus occurred is amongst the finest.

"Trick shot?" Rod enquired as he dropped the ball into Danny's open palm.

"Alright Rod, mate? How you doing?" asked Ray. "Haven't seen you in a while."

"Fine thanks Ray. Lager? Dan – lager?"

In time, Rod would come to realise what a ridiculous question that was.

"Two lagers and the usual for me please, Sean."

Sean looked down at Rod – it wasn't just the difference in height, it was just the manifestation of the general contempt in which he held everybody.

"So, two lagers and what?" he mumbled just loud enough for Rod to hear.

"Two lagers and a cider. Pint. Cheers."

Sean poured the drinks from the other end of the bar, musing on how his clientele had just increased by fifty per cent with Rod's arrival. Well, more or less fifty per cent he thought. And then he smirked, unnoticed by the others. Smiling caused a physical pain – a smirk was just manageable.

"What's up with Sean?" asked Rod.

"Can't wash his skanky joggers," replied Ray, chalking his cue as if he were trying to grind it into the ground. "Anyway Rod. Do you play?"

"Play what?"

"Pool. This." Ray gesticulated towards the pool table as if he had just produced it from a cloud of smoke. "Do you play pool?"

Rod smiled, rolled up the sleeves of his shirt and plucked a cue from the rack.

"Any chalk?" he enquired.

Ray handed him a worn piece of cue chalk and Rod proceeded to chalk his cue with it, blowing off the excess, creating a beautiful pale blue dust cloud that glimmered in the green glare of the lights that hung precariously over the pool table.

"So who's up then?" asked Rod.

"I'll give you a game."

It was Little Jon calling out from the other side of the pub. He had just walked in and was waiting for Sean to re-appear so he could get a drink.

"Is he any good?" Rod asked Ray.

Ray nodded.

"I guess we'll see," replied Rod, blowing more chalk off the top of his cue and walking through the bluedust, all Lawrence of Arabia and manic smurf miner.

Now pool isn't just a game of balls and pockets and green baize and silence. It is so much more than that. It's the bending over and the pulling slowly back and the whacking and the smacking and the beauty beauty dropping into the deep dark holes of the corner cornering. It's the softly safety and the angle of the spangle and the wavering light of the wavering sight. It's the admission of guilt, the culmination of nations and the final overpowering of the ciderings and the absolute beauty of mathematics in a pub that knows nothing but perfect, perfect desperations. It is the clack, clack of balls and the shakes of the head of wonderful people.

Little Jon wasn't particularly little – certainly not in comparison to Rod. And the sobriquet hadn't been applied in an ironic fashion either. Actually, as with so many nicknames, the story of its origin had become somewhat vague and fragmented over the years. But what hadn't changed was his singular style of attire which consisted primarily of tucking one or other of his collection of plain V-neck jumpers into his jeans. Many a girlfriend (and there had been a few!) had stood aghast as he had steadfastly refused to listen to her fashion advice. And many a relationship had burst asunder on the rocks of his idiosyncrasies – tucking his jumper into his jeans being but one of them.

"Hello mate. I'm Jon."

Jon walked over to Rod and shook his hand.

"Rod."

"Alright lads?" asked Jon of Ray and Danny.

"As ever mate," replied Danny.

"Oh yes," said Ray, smiling. For Ray, having a friend meeting another of his friends for the first time was almost like seeing a plan come together, a fine, wonderful plan whose unspoken and unwritten aim was to see all the population of the world at least acknowledge one another on a first name basis if one person was to see another in passing. He felt, with Little Jon having now met Rod, a sense of accomplishment. Todd Snider had once sung about being 'the world's best friend' – and undoubtedly Todd Snider was the perfect candidate for such a role - but if ever he did wear that crown it would be thanks to some bloke called Ray from The Setting Sun in Chelmsford.

So Little Jon and Rod Langford played their game of pool, a game that the former won, though not as easily as he won most games. His ability to utter a well-timed phrase just as his opponent lined up a simple pot was legendary. Such statements usually incorporated phrases like 'you've won this now', 'you could pot that with my cock' or 'sometimes the luck's with you mate and sometimes it isn't.' Such interjections had led to the odd confrontation in the past when money was at stake or the other player rose to the bait. And Little Jon was not great with confrontation. That's where Ray would act as peacemaker, apologising for his friend, buying the other bloke a drink and generally saving the world. In years gone by he would have just punched the nearest person but these days, well, he just read the right books.

"Don't worry, Rod," commiserated Danny as Little Jon potted an easy black one handed whilst looking in the opposite direction. "Two pints and he won't be able to stand up. Give him a game then."

Rod smiled at Danny and looked over at Little Jon who, having put down his cue in victory, was in the process of ensuring his jumper was fully wedged into his jeans. The ensuing hours were filled with banter and quiet moments, drunken games of pool, Ray pulling the back of Little Jon's jumper unnoticed from the back of his jeans and generally four Englishmen just doing their best to get through the night.

None of them saw Eryn Rose and Brando at the table in the beer garden. When the lads were playing pool they would smoke outside the front of the pub as it was closer. Brando would come in and order drinks occasionally but Eryn Rose stayed outside. Sean eyed them with suspicion and he served Brando with reluctance. Just as some people have a heightened sense of foreboding, so Sean had a great intuition for goodness. And he didn't like what he saw in these two. He didn't like it at all. Goodness always made him reach for his darts.

"So have you calmed down a bit now, Brando?" asked Eryn Rose, all passion compassion.

"It's not about calming down. It's about fairness," replied Brando. "I've got just as much right to be an angel as you. I was all lined up to do that Tollesbury job and that was taken away from me. If I hadn't brought you this midget referral I'd be in Tollesbury now sorting that nurse out. And now I'm just playing sidekick to you. And that midget, that Rod, I could have handled him – no problem. Except now I'm left to play marriage guidance or whatever it is I'm supposed to do with his wife. How fair do you think all that is?"

He drank a good half of the pint he had just ordered, sighed and looked around him, despising the drabness of the beer garden and the very fact he knew Eryn Rose would have all the answers.

"I wish you wouldn't refer to Rod as 'the midget.'"

"Oh ok. So now you have to be politically correct to be an angel. At least now I know where I was going wrong."

Eryn Rose closed her eyes for a moment.

"Please Brando. You will make a wonderful angel. I know it. Rod's wife does genuinely worry me. It wouldn't surprise me if you'd been assigned to her because she is more challenging than the nurse in Tollesbury. Had you considered that?"

Brando looked at Eryn Rose wondering if she was being serious or whether she was just humouring him. Wherever the truth lay, he really didn't have many cards to play.

"None of this is about us," continued Eryn Rose. "It's about doing what we can for other people, strangers, people we've never met and will never meet again. The whole angel organisation is just that – helping other people get through whatever they're going through. And everybody is going through something. It's not like there will ever be a shortage of cases. Getting your wings is the hardest thing. After that it's just about using them."

But knowing deep inside the difference between right and wrong is the easy part – as is deciding each morning when you get up that this will be the day when you begin your life of purity. From this moment on I will think no thoughts of condemnation, I will speak no words of condemnation and I will commit no acts of condemnation. Ah they are words on which we all should surely feast the very moment we awake. Yes we need our coffee and our bran and our wheat and our milk, but to affirm goodness just has to be the mightiest of meals to begin the day. But how swiftly do our thoughts and our words and our actions disintegrate! By lunchtime we are in need of replenishment. By the evening we have rationalised the events of our day. And during the night our thoughtdreams will just not leave us alone.

Compassion is the natural human condition. When we are hungry our stomach informs us with a growl. When we are thirsty our throat gives us a dry and scratchy warning. When we are lacking in compassion, reason deceives us into believing that life has a logic to it. Don't fall for it people. Eat when you're hungry, drink when you're dry and give love wherever you go!

65

LOGIN - ROD
PASSWORD *******
FILE
OPEN "WIDEAWAKE"

Now here's a thing. Seems I'm now in The Setting Sun Pool Team. Met Little Jon today. Seems he doesn't usually lose. But then he hasn't had the practice I've had. He's never been inside, far as I know. I've never seen anyone get so pissed so easily. He was only on Fosters as well. I know I only beat him near the end but still I don't think the lads will let him forget it. So funny how he has his jumper in his trousers. I think he thinks it makes him look cool. Funny fucker.

When I told Liz about the Pool Team she didn't seem too bothered. Said it was nice I'd have something to do every Monday. She's been well quiet lately. Must be her job. I'd hate to do what she does. Then, funny thing, she asked me if I'd seen some bird on a swing the other day at the park down the bottom of the flats. Told her she must have been doing one too many nights. It's not that I'm worried about her – she's a strong old girl. Cope with anything Liz could. She doesn't think like I do, which I reckon is one of the things that helps her. I think sometimes I've paid the price for thinking too much.

When I do what I'm gonna do, when I kill in the way I will, yeah, Liz will be upset for a couple of days maybe, but she'll carry on. She may even make a bit of money out of the whole thing – interviews with the papers and on the telly and stuff. I'll see her right. I'm that sort of bloke.

I've noticed lately that I've begun to divide people up. When I came out of prison it didn't bother me who it was I chose to kill. Having met the lads though - Ray, Danny, Alex and Little Jon - I can see now that not everyone deserves it. That's why I have to be selective, you see. I've come to the conclusion that by killing I should also be doing good. I know that sounds weird but that's what I'm thinking. To do good by doing bad seems to fit with me right now. That one will make the reporters think. I might even turn out to be like a hero or something. This whole murder thing will take a bit more thinking about. Like I said. It's just the details now I need to finalise. I've got the will and the power. Never been any doubt about that.

Bird on a swing. What sort of bird goes on a kid's swing in a dossy little park anyway? And upsets my Liz in the process. Sort of bird that needs killing maybe? Who knows? It's me that has the decision to make, me that will hold the knife that will cut the puppet strings of whoever it is I choose to take down.

SAVE

8. Arborist, Buddhist, Pacifist And Wonderfulest

Ray and Danny – or Mr Simpson and Mr Slater as they were better known to the pupils of King Charles Secondary School in Chelmsford – were teachers, educators of this country's children, purveyors of knowledge and ideals, surrogate parents of the disaffected North Essex youth of our times. Danny taught economics – a fact which was often the source of much mirth amongst his friends considering his enduring financial predicaments. Ray taught history. If ever a man was born to teach history, it was Ray; a man for whom every moment mattered, every person counted and every act was significant.

"Getting the team together tonight, Dan. Final practice before the kick-off on Monday. What time you gonna get there?"

"About eight I reckon. I've got to do your bloody after-school idiots computer class haven't I?"

The two friends sat in the cramped staff room, Miss Blake, a crestfallen Geography teacher the only other person present. She gazed out of the single grimy window, looking down at the playground in which the children played so joyously, wondering whether it was her or her subject that was responsible for the dissipation of all their fun between the hours of ten and eleven every morning.

"Come on, mate," said Ray. "You do owe me one, remember? That old 'Henry the Eighth had a brother called Eric who was a plumber' debacle? And all those kids moaning at me, telling me Mr Slater said they should definitely mention 'Eric' in the exam paper? You owe me big time for that mate."

Danny chuckled to himself. Not that he had chuckled much when he had received his final written warning from the headmaster.

But, he had decided, the whole thing had been worth it. Pupils, as far as he was concerned, should be taught to question and to explore, not to just remember and repeat by rote without ever fully understanding. The headmaster hadn't bought this defence. Ray had taken a while to get over the fact that his best friend could be so damn funny.

"So where's your laptop, Ray? Has it got all the stuff on it?"

"Yeah. Just switch it on before you plug it into the white board thing otherwise you'll be able to see everything on the laptop but not on the white board. Or maybe it's the other way round. Not sure. You'll work it out."

"Cheers mate," replied Danny. "See you down the pub. Never been in a pool team before. Got to hand it to you. Exciting times!"

"Absolutely!"

The classroom where Danny was due to teach the children who had expressed an interest in the basic computer class was gloomy and dull. One of the fluorescent lights didn't work and the blinds on the windows could either be fully closed or fully open – any attempt to have them at half mast would lead to the blinds rolling up rapidly to the top of the window with the snapping sound of a thousand cap guns. Danny decided it would best if the blinds were left closed – partly due to the fact that he would be projecting from his laptop to the white board on the wall but mainly to prevent the group of nefarious youths who would undoubtedly gather at the windows, ridiculing the few inside who actually wanted to learn something.

There were nine children in total, all new to the school and all eleven years old. What drew them together was the decision they had individually taken that they would rather be at school than be at home. As a child may prefer school to home so a parent may decide that having a child was a mistake for which they will pay for the rest of their lives. And when a child comes to know that of their own mother or their own father, well, there is an emotion created that bubbles and boils from the depths of that small person that may one day give rise to either a great love for humanity or a hatred of those that feel any love at all. People like Danny Slater and Ray Simpson give such children a chance to realise that they have choices in their lives, that nothing is ordained and that they can indeed have a say in what happens to them. And I bloody love them for it.

There are heroes all over this earth. All over. And I don't care what you say – heroes don't carry guns. A true hero carries compassion in his heart and forgiveness in his soul. That's all. He sweeps the streets of your town and he delivers your post. He drives your trucks and he sleeps in your shop doorways. You pass him in the street and wonder why he says good morning to you even though you don't even know him. And as you walk on further you will maybe smile to yourself and look back over your shoulder at that stranger who just made your day. You don't see the glow but my god you feel it - and startled, you will realise that your life just got that little bit more wonderful.

"Right," said Danny, opening up the laptop and plugging it into the big white board behind him. "Mr Simpson has asked me to do this with you today as he has other engagements. Alright?"

Two of the boys said "yes sir", three nodded, three more just stared ahead whilst one lone child at the back of the room just fiddled with the temperamental blinds on the window beside him.

"If we could leave those blinds alone Jordan, that would be good."

Jordan hung his head and fiddled with his hair instead, perhaps half hoping for a tugged curl to precipitate the rolling up of his entire being, leading him to disappear with a pop into complete nothingness.

"Not a problem, Jordan mate. Just you know what those twats outside are like. Can't stand school but can't be bothered to go home either," reassured Danny who was entirely unaware of the poignancy of the statement he had just made.

The boys watched as the white-board at the front of the classroom lit up with the Microsoft Windows logo. Danny typed in the password and looked behind himself just to make sure all was working correctly. So far so good. Within an hour he would be down

The Setting Sun with his mates, pint in hand and pool practice ahead of him. How many children realise that those who teach them at times have such thoughts in their mind, such desires? Young or old, we're all just trying to get through this crazy life.

"So, boys. I know it's your first term here so I should imagine you've already been bombarded with all the rules and regulations and obviously you would have worked out that without a computer your studies are going to be fairly difficult. If you haven't got access to a computer at home, you will have to use the ones in the library here or the library in town and the way things are these days if you don't know how to use a computer you've pretty much had it, whether it be your school work or in terms of getting a job when you leave school. So we're going to start with the basics. All good?"

All still awake. Sometimes that's as good as it gets.

"Just to let you know there are six parts to this course and usually it won't be me taking you - it'll be Mr Simpson. He devised all the lessons and he's kind of in charge of the whole thing. It's just he couldn't make it this afternoon."

Some of the boys nodded and some smiled. Some did both. The boy Jordan had his hands clasped between his knees to stop him fiddling with anything – except perhaps his knees.

"So," continued Danny. "What you can see on the screen behind me is what is on this laptop screen. It's the basic screen you get when you turn the computer on. You'll have various pictures called icons that if you double-click them – which basically means pressing the left mouse button twice, they will take you through to a specific programme."

As Danny was reading from the pre-prepared print-out in front of him, it all sounded more complicated than it actually needed to. Another twenty minutes or so and he would be in his car, one more day done. That's what his teaching life had become – just a counting down of the days. But counting down to what? Just the next one. That was all. Just the next one. His alcohol consumption had become in some way a protective factor that served to inject reminiscence into

71

his memory of what once was and inhibit his fears of what may be to come. Now that's not so bad in some ways. But when your job hangs upon the ticking of boxes and the filling in of forms, ideals and spirit sadly carry but little weight.

"What I'm going to do now is to double-click on this icon here – the one for Microsoft Outlook. This is where my emails are stored. Got it? Yours might not be in Outlook. They will be with whoever you have your email account but for this demonstration they're in Outlook."

More and more complicated. Time ticking by. Lager on tap and the chalk awaiting the cue. The boys looked on, thinking who knows what. They weren't asking any questions and for Danny that was a bonus. Just read the lesson plan and get out.

"Right. All still alive?"

Danny had been told many times over the years that continuously checking the well-being of the children he taught was bordering upon an affliction for which the modern day professional teacher was more or less impelled to seek help.

The pupils at King Charles' Secondary School generally loved Danny – particularly the new pupils. There was something about his manner that made them feel more like children. And when you're eleven, that's exactly how you should feel.

"Good. So here's my email thing, well not mine exactly, one set up for this lesson. So because that one is in bold lettering it means it's a new email. I just click on it and it will then open."

Danny double-clicked beautifully, with precision, finesse and with a shot of conviction that convinced him that he was actually helping children in a practical, wonderful way. Yep, he double clicked that mouse like he had never double-clicked a mouse before. And then he wished he hadn't.

He wasn't sure what he heard first – the initial yelp of laughter, a boy choking on his chewing gum or the snapping of the blind that had finally given way to Jordan's fiddling which had somehow not just released the blind on the window beside him, but all the other blinds on all the other windows. Wonderful. Technology at its best. From laptop screen to letters three feet high, all perfectly visible to the oiks outside who were now pressed up against the windows, banging on them, hooting and roaring and collapsing like dominoes to the ground.

MR SLATER IS A PEADO.

MR SLATER IS A PEADO.

MR SLATER IS A PEADO.

Danny pressed every button on the keyboard with, it must be said, an alarming lack of finesse, but the buoyant words remained. In vain he closed the lid of the laptop but of course the image continued to flash its message.

"Jordan! Pull down that blind now!" Danny shouted. Jordan did as he was told then sat on the floor continuing to giggle as if he was having the most enjoyable seizure ever.

The boys finally stood up and left the room without even being asked. In one sense they had learned a valuable lesson about the power of computers, but much more significantly that moment, for many of them, would be recounted in years to come as *the* memory of their school days, in some fine way masking the years of tears and the lonely walks and the backward glances and the deep, deep sighs that truly encapsulated the supposed finest years of their fledgling lives. Danny, well, he had learned that Eric the Plumber was perhaps even more dangerous than his bearded, more corpulent elder brother.

And somewhere up a tree there is Alex Milne – Arborist, Buddhist, Pacifist and Wonderfulest. He's doing what he does in his day job, protecting the green and touching up the edges of the scene. So as we pass the foliage and the shrubbery serene at our hundred miles an hour speed, still just a swathe of the beauty of the breathing depths of this earth is visible amidst the watercolour wash of our hurry and our scurry.

Whilst Danny had his head in his hands and Alex had his head in the clouds, Little Jon was spinning metaphorical plates. As a nurse at Broomfield Hospital, Chelmsford, his days were long indeed. He would go from bed to bed, from family to family and from highs to lows and back again. His limbs would weary but his heart never did. Desperate questions, pleading eyes and sighs, sighs, sighs were the threads of his working life. The times he was able to nip out the back for a forbidden cigarette were more about breaking the rules than sparking the fag. When the plates you spin have the propensity to break as easily as a human heart then you just can't do without an inhalation of rebellion.

The real wars are not fought on battleships and frontlines, in bunkers or in foxholes – they are fought in wards and hospices and surgeries - theatres of compassion – not theatres of war. Little Jon wore his name badge like a Victoria Cross and he would hurl his spent cigarette across the car park as if it were a grenade before immersing himself once more in the provision of hope to those who have lost all sight of that most tortuous of paradigms. He had a smile for everyone and a joke for any that would listen. They were generally crap jokes but at least they were jokes.

That Monday night Little Jon managed to get off on time, for once, and drive as fast as fast in his BMW wowzer machine. He had once made The Essex Arms in Brentwood to Dukes Night Club in Chelmsford within nine minutes. There was something about only just staying in control that gave him the buzz of buzzes. But he didn't know then, as he careered around the Miami Roundabout, The Setting Sun in sight, how close he was to falling off the very edge of this world.

But you have to laugh and not take it all soooo seriously. There's so little in this life we can control, so little that we can truly influence. And when we're tired and we're drunk and we're crazy and distraught we have choices which include whether to go on, stand still or just hideaway in our hideaway, our cupboard under the stairs that beckons with its cool darkness and its fragrance of mis-remembered summer holidays long past. Curl up and breathe deep my friends in the womb of your own devising. But don't ever remain there. Pop out relieved and refreshed and bouncing back into the game - for the world only turns because of people like you.

And thus it was inevitable that Danny would walk into the pool room of The Setting Sun that evening with Ray, Alex, Little Jon and Rod clapping slowly and intoning with grinning Gregorian chant perfection the words "Peado. Peado. Peado. Peado…"

9. Tattoos On The Back Of Your Calves

Liz Langford had been born in St John's Hospital, Chelmsford in May 1977. She was the only child of an only child and passed her early years in earnest silence. Her parents communicated with her through small gestures and gesticulations. She didn't speak a word until she was three and a half years old. There had just been no need. Disappointment can be conveyed by a raised eyebrow or a deep sigh, disillusionment by the shake of the head. You don't need to be able to verbalise your thoughts to know that.

The house in which she grew up was more home to a frown than ever it was to a smile or a cuddle. There was a delicacy that permeated every movement, a precision that ensured doors were shut with a click and towels were folded without unduly troubling the surrounding air.

It wasn't that her parents disliked Liz or consciously abused her. It was just they they did not know what they should do. They read books on the art of parenting. They watched television programmes about parenthood. And they spoke long into the night about what approach would be best to ensure 'the child' developed in as correct a fashion as possible. All the while Liz would be in her bedroom surrounded by pink and fluff but feeling just blue and cold. It was nobody's fault. No-one was to blame. It just was. That's all.

Early birthdays were attended by several children who were friends of friends of her parents. As time wore on, Liz had grown used to the fact that a birthday is merely a marker of how many years you have managed to endure. They served ultimately as an annual confirmation to her that her place was on the edge of all things. In just a few short years a bouncy castle had become a trip to McDonalds with her mum and dad – burgers and fries picked at in silence.

As you can imagine, school was something of a shock to Liz Langford. She attended the Anglo-European School in Ingatestone which was about a seven mile bus ride from where she lived with her parents in the Moulsham Lodge area of Chelmsford. It had grown from the restructuring of Ingatestone Secondary Modern and was officially renamed in 1973. In 1977 it became the first English school to offer the International Baccalaureate Diploma and was thus considered an educational establishment of note. The fact that Liz's father had spent three years working abroad in Spain, advising on the setting up of a particular type of hedge fund, was sufficient for Liz to meet the entry requirements.

The school consisted of large, sprawling buildings that spread out before a lonely, quiet child like the side of a mountain. You were either meant to be there or you weren't. You fitted in or you flitted out. And if you were somewhere in between it would take you most of your schooling life before you were eventually compelled to acknowledge the fact that your childhood had truly been and gone. It was the kind of school where there were cliques instead of gangs – to be excluded from the former was no less dangerous to the developing psyche of a child than being chased by the latter. At least if you're chased you can run. But when you're excluded, well where is there to stumble but into the dull confines of your own stunned mind?

Growing up is a process during which you are given the opportunity to learn how the adult world works before you become a part of it. If you're lucky, you make mistakes and learn that it's okay to make mistakes. You meet good people, have solid love around you and achieve what psychiatric assessments in future years will refer to as 'the necessary milestones.' You will have your difficult times of course but they won't dominate, won't overwhelm. They will contribute to the formation of a healthy caution within your defences that will ensure you sail through your formative years and early adulthood with relative ease.

But what of those who do become overwhelmed, who know, truly KNOW, so early on that they do not fit? You've seen them as have I. Their school jumpers just hang a little too loose from the elbows and there is a darkness, a subtle smudge beneath the eyes that is far beyond their years. No matter how often they wash their hair it always has a certain sheen to it that will not go away.

So that was Liz – empty, incomplete, bereft of the pinnacles of emotion of which childhood should comprise. There was no running up the stairs and slamming of the bedroom door, no falling madly in love with a boy band boy and no storming rows or suicidal inclinations. She wasn't abused and she wasn't a bully. She didn't seek thrills nor did she recoil from them. They were just never within her reach, even had she known of them. You may think that such a childhood, free from extremes would produce a well-adjusted adult. Wishful thinking, people. Wishful thinking.

Brando checked the photograph once more as he sat on the ground outside Wilkos, his back to the wall. Thomas The Tank Engine was rocking back and forth beside him, a bemused child hanging on for dear life whilst its father was having an irate conversation on his mobile phone, stepping further and further away in order to distance himself from the nauseating tune.

"How many more times do I have to tell you? They didn't have any courgettes."

A pause.

"How was I supposed to know a cucumber isn't any good? They look the fucking same."

Thomas The Tank Engine eased to a stop, the child continued to wail and the man hung up on his wife.

In days long gone Brando may well have lit himself a cigarette at this point, but since he had finally been given the opportunity to be an angel, he had tried to stop smoking. Not that giving up the fags made him any more likely to be accepted as an angel – it wasn't even one of the requirements – not smoking just made him feel 'purer', more angel-like. It was difficult to explain and he was thankful that he never had to. His mentor, Renbourne, had barely communicated with him since the last meeting since post-it notes were outlawed. Despite his initial feelings, he was growing to accept that Renbourne did indeed know what he was doing. He was more than a little uptight and entirely full of himself but, considered Brando, if anyone had a right to such unedifying characteristics it was the foremost member of the Eastern Region Angel Collective.

Liz Langford was entirely unaware that a novice angel was waiting for her to finish her shift. The parameters of her life had ever been narrow and neither angel nor devil had previously felt the need to ripple the dank pool of her burgeoning ennui.

And there she was all deep breaths and rolling hips, eyes to the ground and arms swinging a little more than they rightly needed to. She propelled herself like a clockwork doll, oblivious to all that surrounded her, having learned from early on that to subject yourself to that which you do not understand is an unnecessary punishment.

Brando scrambled rather inelegantly to his feet and began to follow his target. Liz walked passed the Wilkos garage and stood at the dual carriageway some distance from the crossing point. She observed the cars as they hurtled towards her and imagined what it would feel like to be hit by one of them. She thought of the chances of survival and decided she would be one of the 'lucky ones' who would pull through with broken limbs and the memory of her life intact. She waited for a reasonable space to present itself, made for the central reservation and then walked on over to the other side of the road that bordered Trinity Park. Brando caught up with her just as she stepped onto the pavement, having narrowly avoided being clattered into by a Ford Fiesta that had evidently seen better days more clearly than it had seen Brando.

"Hello. Liz Langford? Sorry, can I just quickly talk to you?"

Liz had barely heard him. She was no longer at work and she wasn't home yet. There were no obligations upon her to interact with the world. Her journey to and from Wilkos was conducted in a bubble of her own devising, a burble that would only ever burst on the odd occasion when Rod would meet her half-way to home as a gesture of something or other. But when she felt a hand upon her round shoulder she couldn't help but come to a halt. She didn't gasp. She didn't even look round. She just waited for whatever was next.

"Sorry. It's alright. I just need to talk to you," continued Brando, stepping around to stand in front of Liz. She seemed so much smaller when she was standing still. Her locomotive piston motion had lent a stature to her that was absent when she had run out of steam. Brando's hand upon her shoulder had stopped her in her well-worn tracks. She could still feel his finger tips upon her even now as he spoke, though their contact had been but fleeting.

Liz looked up at Brando, resigned and barely interested. For all she cared he could punch her in the face and steal her empty purse. She had never been punched before and wondered what it would feel like. There was a power in her expression that may have caused a more intuitive being than Brando to have apologised and gone on his way. But Brando had something to prove, a mission to complete. It's not every day you get the chance to become an angel.

"I know this sounds really mad, but do you mind if I walk with you for a while? There are some things I think you should know."

And so it was that clear afternoon that Liz Langford found herself sitting on a bench beside a stranger in Trinity Park, wondering if this moment would precipitate the beginning or the end of her life. Part of her really didn't care one way or the other. But there is a spark in all of us - for good or for ill - a spark just waiting to be fanned into a fire of creative inspiration or into the flames of destruction.

Whilst Liz sat on the park bench waiting for Brando to explain to her why she had been accosted, so Eryn Rose at last had Rod within her sights. She was swinging on her new favourite swing when she saw her diminutive quarry stumble out of the door of the block of flats to her left. She watched as he tried to regain his cool and she smiled as she leapt from the swing when it was at its wowest highest point. She stretched her arms out wide on landing, bowed to an invisible audience and skipped into the street.

Eryn Rose always sang a little louder than she was realised. She loved to sing, particularly when the days were long and bright. The ting-a-ling notes that danced haphazard from her pretty red mouth blended with the summer air as if the sky were an orchestral movement. So light were her feet upon the ground that it was her gentle sing-songing that caused Rod to stop and turn. And when he did, an angel was there to greet him.

"Hello!"

Rod looked up. For Eryn Rose was a little taller than him.

"Yeah?"

"Do you mind if I walk with you for a while?"

Eryn Rose's innate spirit beauty prettiness drifted towards Rod so purely it almost took form.

"If you like," he replied. "I'm only going up the road though."

"That's fine!"

Eryn Rose ceased skipping and walked alongside Rod, matching his short steps as best she could. The sun was high in the cloudless blue sky and skipping was always her choice of motion - but there is always a time for even an angel to rein it all in a little, to appreciate for just a while what it must be like not to have wings; even if those wings are just tattoos on the back of your calves.

"So how did you get on?" asked Eryn Rose later that evening, her eyes closed as she licked her ice-cream softly and slowly.

"Not bad," replied Brando. "Told her I worked for these people who make sure people who have got in trouble stay out of trouble. Like probation, but better. I think she got it."

"What are your plans?"

"Said I'd see her every couple of weeks so I can make sure Rod's doing alright. She seemed to accept it."

"What did she say?"

"Nothing. Just kept looking at me."

"In what way?"

"Like she'd never seen a human being before in her life, to be honest. Interested but disappointed all at the same time. Sort of creeped me out."

Eryn Rose opened her eyes and looked at her would-be angel colleague.

"Take care when you're with her, Brando. I'm beginning to think maybe, well. Who knows how all this is going to turn out? But you take care, you hear me?"

Brando dismissed her pleas with an expression of which Sean the miserable landlord would have been proud. "So what are your plans with Rod?"

"We're going to meet in the beer garden at The Setting Sun and work out a plan from there. I told him I've got something to tell him that will change his life. He didn't say he would be there but he didn't say he wouldn't. I think he'll come. I mean, who doesn't want to change their life?"

"You've got ice-cream on your nose," said Brando.

"I know," replied Eryn Rose - as if it were the most normal thing in the world.

Rod and Liz sat opposite one another at their small fold-out flat-pack dinner table for two. Jasmine the dog lay on its back with its legs in the air. Its eyes glistened and widened whenever Liz looked over. The TV was on with the sound turned right down and the computer by the door hummed, a red and green screensaver ball bouncing erratically within the confines of the monitor screen. The beech tinted laminate flooring was rendered almost white in places by the late afternoon sun that lit upon the single bay window, the bay itself doubling as the dining area for the flat's two diminutive occupants.

"You alright then?" Rod asked. "Shepherd pie's nice," he added.

Liz nodded. Her husband was unsure as to whether the nod signified his wife was 'alright' or whether it was an acknowledgement of the recognised quality of the meal she had prepared for them both.

"Did you do anything different with it?"

Liz wanted to say that she'd shaken it up before putting it in the microwave or that its sell by date was three weeks ago, but she just couldn't be bothered. So she just smiled instead, the sort of smile where the lips are drained of colour and lose all their potent elasticity.

"You're well quiet," Rod persisted. "Is it the job?"

Putting her knife and fork into the centre of her empty plate, Liz looked directly at Rod. She thought his eyes a little small in comparison to Brando's and his face lacked the symmetry that Brando's possessed.

"I'm ok. Just tired that's all," she managed.

And for reasons neither could possibly articulate, no mention was made of their respective encounters earlier that day with complete strangers, encounters that would prove more significant for all the participants than any of them could ever have imagined.

10. The Jimpsies Of This Land

Pubs aren't like football teams. Although there can certainly be a degree of loyalty to your favourite pub it rarely spills over into feelings of animosity for another pub in the same area. As Ray had inferred in his pleas to Sean with regard to starting up the pool team, someone might walk into one pub representing his own establishment and, following a wonderful evening of bonhomie, fine ale, great music and a genuine feeling of belonging, that person may then become a regular of that pub, eschewing the previous one as quickly as it would take to swap a red and blue scarf for a white one.

"Right," said Ray, his team around him. "We've got four singles games and two doubles. Ideally there'd be eight of us but we'll just have to make do. Dan, you have the first game. Get it out the way. I'll have the next one, then you Alex, then Rod and Little Jon. For the doubles it'll be me and Alex and then Jon and Danny."

"So I'm going first, then last?"

"Yeah. Get your nerves sorted with the first one then storm the last one with Little Jon here."

"But you know I'll be mullered by the time the last game comes round. I'll sort the nerves out with drink then won't be able to stand to hold my cock let alone a pool cue."

"Just go easy tonight mate. Just for one night. Come on."

"Lager?" Danny asked the team.

The team, including Ray, replied in the affirmative.

And that was when Rod sauntered in, his recently purchased charity shop cue held in his hands like an AK-47, mowing the lads down whilst making rat-a-tat-tat sounds that instantly took every man within twenty yards back to their school playground war days - arms linked, gathering members with each step chanting: "Who wants to play WAR? Who wants to play WAR?" And by the time every child had decided they did want to play WAR, the bell would go and the long line of linked children would disperse, disappointed but unwounded, adrenaline high but limbs intact.

The team from the Eagle and Hind walked in just as The Setting Sun lads were well into their first pints.

Rod picked up his cue again, an excited grin on his face, and pretended once more that it was a gun – this time aiming it at the opposition.

"He one of yours?"

It was the dour captain of the Eagle and Hind, gesturing in Rod's direction but looking straight at Ray.

"He is," replied Ray, putting his pint on the bar and standing straight and proud. He motioned for Rod to come and join the lads. "He's up first. Start in ten minutes if that's alright with you, Graham."

But Graham wasn't listening. He and his team were being served almost within seconds by a smiling Sean. Alex almost betrayed his permanent gentle Buddha visage and had Danny seen that smile on the usually miserable Landlord he may well have spat out his first drop of alcohol in twenty years.

"First?" queried Rod. "Are you sure?"

"You've got your own cue, haven't you?" said Ray, nodding down at what was now most definitely a piece of wood with chalk on the end and not an AK-47.

"Yeah, but first? I've not even had time to warm up."

"Nor have those fuckers. Do you really think Sean would be smiling at them if he wasn't serving them some out of date shit that wasn't going to send them to the bogs quicker than George Michael on a promise? You'll be fine mate. Just take your time. You know what you're doing."

Danny celebrated his relief at not being first up by ordering a whisky chaser and popping a piriton tablet. An old mate of his had once sworn by the combination just before tipping a pint of Guinness over a girl's head in the Essex Arms in Brentwood following a dispute about the Wapping Printing Plant during the Thatcher years.

In The Setting Sun that Monday evening of the game with The Eagle and Hind there were the two sets of players, a couple of disconsolate girlfriends and Derek. Even when Derek wasn't present in the pub, which was seldom, no-one sat on his stool. He would always be the first back you saw when you walked in and the last you saw when you staggered out. It was as if he were a plug and the stool a socket. Together they added a little more life to the place if only as a landmark, a means by which you could find your bearings, stay safe even.

Derek's on his stool. I must be in The Setting Sun. I know where I am. I'll be ok. I'm leaving now. Derek nods goodbye to me as I go even though we've never met before. I do believe he wishes me well.

And Derek has no idea of the effect he has, how safe he makes people feel just by his mere presence. There are people like Derek in every pub in the land. And they are indispensable. They are handed down from generation to generation like a baton of Englishness that will forever be. And if you were ever to tell Derek that, he would just sparkle his eyes at you, shuffle on his stool and smile. Before you knew it, you would have bought him a drink - and he'd have forgotten your name.

Then in walked a man who was Lego made flesh. His stilted gait eschewed the function of knees and ankles and his arms displayed edges where there should have been contours. His head was square and his shiny black hair was surely slotted onto his head by means of a plastic peg. The only glint of being was in the seven earrings that looped through his left ear and the tattoo on his neck that pulsed whenever he breathed.

"Fuck me," Ray said to Danny in a low whisper. "It's Jimpsy."

People stepped back as Jimpsy walked by them and raucous chatter became a mumble. He hadn't been seen in Chelmsford for a good few years.

"Ray, son."

"Alright Jimpsy," replied Ray. "How you doing?"

"Better now you've just bought me a pint."

Ray looked up at Jimpsy and Jimpsy looked down at Ray who in turn looked over at Sean.

"What will it be?" Sean asked.

"The usual," replied Jimpsy.

To everyone's surprise Sean withdrew a bottle of red wine from beneath the bar, filled a pint glass almost to the brim and dropped in a handful of ice-cubes.

Jimpsy's drink cost Ray eleven pounds, money that only enhanced the Landlord's unusually cheerful demeanour. Where his earlier goodwill had been contrived to deceive the visiting pool team that The Setting Sun was a great pub, it seemed that depriving a regular customer of his money as a consequence of that regular customer feeling threatened had ignited within him a joy untold.

Now, Danny had that unfortunate affliction that alcohol imparts upon some people – it made his voice louder and his comments funnier whilst conversely reducing his awareness of consequences. A fine affliction amongst friends, but an acquired taste amongst the Jimpsies of this land.

"So where you been Jimpsy?" asked Danny in all innocence.

"Inside. Six years," replied Jimpsy unblinking, unyielding, sipping his pint of wine, having declined the straw that Sean had offered him – a curly one at that.

Danny mulled over Jimpsy's response and a smile tugged at his lips. He just could not resist. Tony Hancock, Tommy Cooper, Ronnie Barker, Eric Morecambe and Russ Abbott urged him on. Share the laughter! Spread the happiness! Knock 'em dead my son! Ray saw it coming but could do nothing about it but breathe deep and await the explosion.

"Inside for six years? What, are you agoraphobic or something?"

There. It was said. No laughter followed though – canned or otherwise; and happiness seemed something of a leap away. There was just silence. Jimpsy put his pint glass on the bar, his lips stained with the red of the wine. It was as if he had taken a chunk out of an animal and was now supping upon its blood. It was most certainly more than an armful.

"I ain't afraid of no fucking aggro mate," he said, taking a step towards Danny. "Is he a friend of yours Ray?"

Ray nodded.

"Fucking lucky. Bearded fuck."

Alex was about to step in to spread some peace but Ray eyed him away. Little Jon emerged from the toilets, all glee as ever and, as was so often the case, completely oblivious to the subtleties of mood and tension.

"Let's beat these bastards!" he declared, grinning all across his face.

Ray reluctantly bought Jimpsy another pint of wine and a quaking Danny manoeuvred himself to stand behind the one-man civil-rights movement that was Alex.

Outside in Chelmsford the evening darkened and the stars succumbed to the belligerent light of electricity and modernity as they stared into the glare of fazed haze – yet the glimmer does shimmer at the very edges of our wide-eyed and startled vision. A town is just a contracted village and a village is just sticks in a field. And the field? Well, that is just the sea and its offerings. This land of hours, this England, is wonderful beyond mention, gorgeous beyond compare.

And at any one moment, somewhere across this fine country there will undoubtedly be a man tossing a coin whilst others look on.

"Heads," declared Rod.

"Tails. Unlucky."

The chatting stopped and movement slowed. The game was on. There are unwritten rules at such times of which everyone is aware. You don't stand in the eye-line of the player making the shot, you don't talk, you don't cough and you absolutely don't comment unless you're one of the players in that particular game. Nod appreciatively, purse your lips and inhale – even put your hand to your forehead and squint if you like, so long as it's done without pantomime style clown guffaws.

Yet even before Rod took his first shot, someone called out.

"Do you want a stool mate?"

The only noise was of the cling-a-ding-cling-clang of the fruit machine at the other side of the pub.

Rod stood back from the table, took a breath and chalked his cue though he had done so thoroughly just moments before. Ray, however, was primed. Danny retreated behind his beard and Alex closed his eyes. Little Jon giggled. Thirty-four years old and he just couldn't help himself.

"Oi. That's enough."

It was Graham, the Eagle and Hind team captain. Admonishment suitably delivered to his team-member, the room was once again silent – although Little Jon's shoulders still visibly shook over by the bar.

So the match began. Balls clacked and doomphed off of cushions, the green baize breathed and specks of blue chalk partied in the air beneath the pool table lights. Rod started well but his opponent took advantage of a weak long pot and cleared up his remaining yellows. He potted an easy black to win the first game of the match. It was when he patted Rod on the head instead of shaking his hand that it all, as they say, kicked off.

Although these sorts of things are very often a blur for most people involved, it was generally considered that it had been Jimpsy who had been the first to wade in, punching the ungracious winner in the stomach and following it with a hefty shove that flung the doubled-over man into the corner by the dartboard where he succeeded in knocking over a table with two full pints on it.

The immediate response to Jimpsy's actions was for Danny to hide in the toilets lest he be the next recipient of the infamous Jimpsy offensive. Alex shook his head in disappointment at the violence of man and Ray picked up a pool cue with absolutely no intention of chalking it. Rod, who had been pushed out of the way by Jimpsy, found himself by the bar beside Little Jon, who was shaking once more, but in an entirely giggle-free fashion.

Captain Graham stepped towards Jimpsy, his hands out before him in peaceful supplication though his expression bore more a contemptuous sneer than anything approaching amelioration. His face, over the ensuing few days however would exhibit the tell-tale signs of a failed interaction with an angry man who had experienced sneers and contempt far too often to be afraid of any consequences at all – namely bruising around the left eye and a red raw mark upon his cheek courtesy of a big old clumpy ring.

So to say it all 'kicked off' is something of an exaggeration. Basically Jimpsy punched two people, the match was abandoned amidst glares, stares and retreating machismo and Sean declared the fledgling Setting Sun Pool Team disbanded. Jimpsy downed what remained of his pint of wine and strode out, everyone somewhat relieved that he had opened the door first instead of ploughing straight on through it. Ray's cue had gone unused which was perhaps just as well considering the fact that two police officers entered The Setting Sun half an hour later. Graham had been a captain to the end, having phoned in the assaults whilst he and two of his team-mates sat in The Queen's Head down the road talking over what might have been.

"We've had reports of an incident here," said one of the police officers to a clearly bored Sean.

"A report of an assault," clarified his colleague.

After carefully putting down the glass he was drying Sean looked first at one policeman, then at the other.

"You know Jimpsy?" he asked.

They both nodded.

"He smacked a couple of blokes then left not long ago."

"Are the victims still here?"

"No," replied Sean. "They were from The Eagle and Hind. We were playing them in the pool league."

Both policemen turned to look in unison over their respective shoulders.

"At least he opened the door first," remarked one.

"Indeed," replied the other.

What becomes of the Jimpsies of this land? Perhaps they reach a stage in their lives, at whatever age that may be, when they feel their lot is determined. And theirs is not the middle road. It must be either a lifetime of love fulfilled or dwindling years bestriding the barren fields, the glaciers and the ravines wreaking havoc in search of the creator who long since abandoned them in disgust. Fear is a forgotten paradigm. A hardening occurs that is more akin to the production of steel than the freezing of water. There is a permanency about the transformation that will brook no tempering. No heat will thaw the girders of wanton hatred that have replaced the once brittle bones of the wide-eyed and wonderful infant. These people will fill our prisons and our special hospitals, our nightmares and our newspapers, never getting the chance to become the angels they once could have been.

The Setting Sun was left once more to Ray, Danny, Alex and Little Jon. And of course Rod. For he was one of the lads now.

11. A Tingle In The Tangle

LOGIN - ROD
PASSWORD *******
FILE
OPEN "WIDEAWAKE"

A little bit closer now to knowing who I'm going to kill. It's going to be a bloke. Some of those wankers in the pub last night from the other team, well they just made my mind up for me. It won't be one of them – too obvious. Gang revenge and all that. But it'll be a bloke. No doubt about it. Just can't wait to watch him fall, drop like that red should've done that rattled in the jaws of that pocket. Should've gone down. But that's a ball and there's physics and all that, not a person who you can do what you like with. I'm beginning to get excited even writing this.

Got a lock-in last night with the lads. No more pool team but it's kind of brought us closer together. Sean caught Danny helping himself from the optics, told him he was barred. Ray said if you bar Danny you'll have to bar the rest of us. Like the four musketeers we were.

I feel a bit sorry for Jimpsy. Just got out of nick and now probably heading straight back there. Stood up for me though like us lot do – when you've been inside you become kind of like some secret underground club. Not that I couldn't have handled myself, obviously.

Funny, thoughts of killing had gone off my mind for a while. But seeing Jimpsy do what he did, well, it fired me up. Violence can do that. So yeah, it's going to be a bloke. And when I work out who, that's when the fun will start. No doubt about it.

SAVE

Eryn Rose met with Rod two days after the pool team debacle.

"Hi Rod. Thank you so much for coming. I really am pleased!"

Rod sat across from her in The Setting Sun beer garden, the greying slats of a tatty wooden bench between them. There had been something about her during their previous brief encounter. Perhaps it had been her offer to buy him a pint. Perhaps it was the promise of something new.

"Before anything else, I have to read you something and give you my card. Will that be alright? It's just the way we do things."

"We?" Rod enquired, looking over his shoulder and then back at the woman on the other side of the table. He put his pint down as if to further enhance his ability to listen. "What do you mean by 'we'?"

"It will make sense, I promise. Don't be freaked out."

Rod manufactured an expression that was intended to inform the world that nothing could even come close to causing him even a moment of distress. Eryn Rose smiled, having seen that expression so many times before. She withdrew a card from the top pocket of her denim jacket and proceeded to read it to Rod before slipping it across the table to him. Rod took the card and read it again to himself.

My name is Eryn Rose and I am an angel. I have been sent to you in order that your heart and mind may find peace. I cannot tell you how I came to know of you nor who sent me. What I can tell you is that I will do all I can to help you see the wonder of your life. There is no fee involved and no obligation on your part. I am not an affiliate of any religious organisation. I just happen to be an angel who wants to help you.

93

And on the other side of the card, as Rod discovered when he turned it over, were the words:

Eastern Region Angel Collective

As you may imagine, it made no sense at all to Rod and he even had to acknowledge to himself that he was just a little 'freaked out'. For her part Eryn Rose just sat there beaming, looking serene and unimaginably joyous.

"Thanks for the pint," said Rod. "But I don't believe in God."

"God has nothing to do with any of this," replied the angel.

"So what makes you think I want any help?"

"I can't tell you that. I just know that you do."

"Are you police?"

"Nope."

"Probation then. I did all my days. You can't get me on that."

"Let me get you another drink."

Rod downed the rest of his pint, nodded and took out a cigarette. Whilst Eryn Rose was at the bar he smoked in summer silence and looked, for the first time in so long, upwards. Gasps of white powder clouds drifted in and out of the pale blue of the sky and the sun, though it was high and to the west, shone down upon Rod as much as it dared. Three v-shaped birds formed a larger V as they flew steady and sure to the other side of who knows where. And ever so slowly the earth turned upon its axis and seas swelled and trees bent to a breeze that only they could feel. Rod was treated to a glimpse of the true nature of this world in that moment though it presented itself as just a tingle in the tangle of his black unruly hair which he almost, but not quite, mistook for an itch. Whatever had happened, and perhaps because Eryn Rose was pretty and carrying a pint of cider for him, Rod felt more disposed to listen to this strange woman than he had been just a cigarette before.

"Now the way this works," began Eryn Rose, sliding along the bench on her side of the table and placing her pint of cider in front of her, "is that we have four sessions. This isn't the first one. This doesn't count – well it does count, but not as one of the four if you know what I mean. Anyway, on the first session you tell me everything about you, all the bad things that have happened to you, all the bad things you've done and everything that hurts you. You may think you won't say anything as we've just met, but you will, trust me. And that's the other thing – you have to trust me. I'm an angel, remember? And the other three sessions will just be you talking to me. When I get home after each session I will write you a letter. And that's it. I may give you some tasks to complete in between but that is basically it. Four sessions, three letters, a few tasks and we'll see where we are then."

"You won't break me," said Rod firmly. "The judge couldn't break me, prison couldn't break me. You won't break me."

Eryn Rose smiled at the little man in the heavy leather jacket who defied her so. She saw light in his eyes. And where there's light there's a soul and no mistake. That's one of the first things they teach you.

"You're absolutely right Rod. And do you know why?"

"Go on."

"You're already broken aren't you?"

There was nothing he could say because the moment he heard those words he felt Eryn Rose's hand upon his. It was weightless and cool but warm all at the same time. The rest of his body was just a dismal wasteland in comparison to the sensations that now pulsed through his fingers. He didn't know what she was doing to him. All he knew was that he couldn't speak.

Eryn Rose leaned forward and spoke in a low, hum of a voice.

"But we'll fix you, Rod Langford. Or I'm not an angel."

Keeping her right hand upon Rod's left, Eryn Rose picked up her cider, drank it down in one, winked, stood up, slid across an appointment card and left Rod staring at the barren outbuilding whose door had long since been kicked in by the sturdy boot of motherless man.

It was only once she was out in the street and had crossed the road and entered Trinity Park that Eryn Rose felt a little tearful. They were the happiest of tears, the most glorious of tears, the tears you cry when you know you've just done good. And may you ever find reasons to cry.

Brando was yet to have his second meeting with Liz Langford. His initial meeting with her had gone about as well as he had expected it to. Waiting for a woman, following her across the road and then leading her into the park had felt decidedly odd – more to him than to her it seemed. She had accepted his behaviour as if it were normal, as if every day she was accosted in such a fashion. But, as every worn out, run down, bored, dejected and rejected soul knows, there is a thin line between acceptance and resignation. Sometimes resignation isn't due to a specific horrific event in your life, but just to an accumulation of small defeats that gradually tip the balance from hope to hopelessness. And once that balance is tipped there is rarely a way back.

But Brando was new to all this. He believed, at that stage, that Liz was just a particularly trusting person. Eryn Rose was, apparently, never wrong. Well, perhaps in this case, she would be.

When he had fed back the details of his meeting to Renbourne, Brando could tell that his mentor was concerned. It was in the colour of the silence, the density of the air. It may have been insignificant to you or to me but it was there all the same. For all Brando's thoughts about the fact that he had not yet attained the status of angel, he had a grudging respect for the man that had ever had his future in his hands. Eryn Rose had said so often, for as long as Brando could remember in fact, that Renbourne was always right. After all, he wasn't the head of the Eastern Region Angel Collective for nothing.

Becoming an angel had never been something to which Brando had aspired. Most people are brought up to believe that angels are heavenly beings all dressed in white with two large wings on their back and a gold halo floating above their head. We are brought up to believe that angels are inherently religious by nature, their origins stretching back thousands of years. We may be persuaded that angels are nothing more than a relic of tradition, an archaic symbol thrust upon a young child at the insistence of society to ensure that as early as possibly children know of the battle between good and evil. When adolescence brings that paradigm into question, as so often it does, so angels do fall by the roadside, all ragged wings and burned out halos. And that is a tragedy, my friend, for angels are as real as you or I.

When his heart is broken, as Brando's had been eighteen months before his meeting with Liz, a man's life can go either way. Acceptance and resignation again. The only other woman with whom Brando had walked along the street, side by side, since December 2009, had been Eryn Rose – and that was just from Trinity Park to The Setting Sun. So it was that when he had got back home after meeting with Liz that first time his emotions were somewhat all over the place. If asked, he would surely have said that she was by no means a stunner - yet there had been something about her, some kind of power that he had felt. And it had left him feeling uneasy.

On Liz Langford's part, despite her reaction (or lack of it), it wasn't every day that she was led to a park by a tall, dark and handsome stranger. It hadn't taken her long to realise however that it was perhaps she that held the leash. When you've spent most of your life on the edges, watching people, observing their habits and filtering out the incessant noise that accompanies most human beings, your ability to judge fear is much heightened. From the moment Brando had spoken her name, Liz had sensed, at the very least, trepidation – not the trepidation that precedes an act of violence or the culmination of a lifetime of temptation, but the trepidation of one who truly is afraid of himself.

When Rod had gone to prison, Liz had experienced not a sense of fear but a sense of relief. It seemed right that she be on this earth alone. When she had returned home from Chelmsford Magistrates Court she had curled up on the sofa with Jasmine and slept for almost twenty hours. And she had emerged from that foetal warmth in a much refreshed state, calm and unruffled. It was as if during her sleep a power had been conferred upon her, a power born from a final release of any vestige of conscience. *My husband is in prison. That's ok. I no longer know love therefore I can't be hurt anymore. That's ok too.*

Whilst her husband was at The Setting Sun having his hand secured to a weather-beaten picnic table in the concrete beer garden, Liz was in Trinity Park with Jasmine. Though Liz walked with short steps, Jasmine still struggled to keep up with his mistress, his four spindle-legs rotating like white wheels. So intense were his exertions he found himself to be just ahead of Liz as they entered the circular spread of grass that was the focal point of the park. And that was when Jasmine felt a pain around his neck that induced an involuntary yelp from within him. Liz stopped and knelt down beside her little dog who in turn fully expected to be picked up and cuddled. But instead Liz stood up once more and yanked upon the lead. Jasmine yelped again. Liz yanked on the lead again. And Jasmine yelped again.

It is said in some quarters that some dogs have over a hundred different facial expressions. Jasmine had then but one.

12. A Lovelorn English Fool

On the Wednesday morning between Christmas 2010 and New Year 2011 Brando had been sitting tired but optimistic on a hard chair in Stansted Airport awaiting the arrival of the plane that would take him to Dublin. He had taken the cold morning bus in the clear black night with just a small holdall for luggage. The crispness of the air as he had walked from the bus to the terminal had only served to stimulate him at a time when any one of us would perhaps have craved a lovely warm quilt. But Brando was a man on a mission, snapped into life and all set to cross the Irish Sea. The mission: LOVE!

The cramped plane was rammed with hangovers and silent moments and deep down thoughts and a certain inevitability that seemed to propel time just as the engines urged everyone on to the misty Dublin morning that awaited them. There were businessmen, stray family members, deep lost souls and broken-pieced people all with their own stories to tell and lives to lead – the leavings and the goings nobody's business but their own. And Brando was no different. Christmas gone and the new year yet to begin – a limbo, a gap in time where anything seems possible.

There is a positivity in travel that has drawn people on for centuries, something about movement itself that has ever lent hope to an otherwise hopeless situation. People have crossed entire continents to find a safe place to be, to finally settle in peace or to be able to express themselves without recrimination. There are others still who just keep moving, knowing deep inside that it is in the motion itself that true safety lies – there is no commitment in motion, no definition, no judgement and no condemnation. You are on your way to or on your way from. You are travelling and that is all. Hope deserves to be that simple. Just writing these lines makes me want to pack a bag and head out into this starlit Tollesbury night and see just where it will take me. Undoubtedly though I would not make it any further than The King's Head. Then I will return home; for perhaps already I am in heaven.

Brando disembarked and made his way through Dublin airport and out into the grey white morning. He eschewed the line of taxis for the designated coach-stop. He was heading for a small village named 'Hook' - and that was all he knew. Love would see him right. The fog told him so, the heavy clouds told him so and his beating English heart told him so. What more confirmation could a young man need? But he was in Ireland – a country where even the deepest, most throbbingest heart of the most gentle and lovingest of Englishman has oft failed to be heard.

The Bus Eireann arrived just before 07.30 and Brando made his way to the back and shuffled across to be by the window, pressing his face against the cold glass. Outside, the sodden mist welled up around the feet of the business-like and the strange, the sanguine, the weary and the bereft. The bus filled slowly until almost half the seats were taken. Then with a sigh of its doors it eased off into the early morn.

Before long Brando's mind settled upon the reason for his journey. Her name was Rosanne and he was in love with her. It was a recent love, for sure, but a love nonetheless. He had split with his wife in November and met Rosanne in December. Just a few weeks later he was leaving England for the first time in his twenty-nine years. As the window began to fill with the dewy green fields of the cold Irish day, Brando felt a surety he had known but few times in his life. Years of an unfortunate, ill-timed, though well-intentioned, marriage had led him to an emerald awakening, the fulfilment of which was just a bus-ride, a hike and a phone-call away.

The hike part of the journey came quicker than Brando had imagined. The rudimentary instructions he had printed out the night before seemed to be as optimistic as the man for whom they were intended. As it was, either he had got on the wrong bus or the route had changed. But love doesn't panic. Love accepts and adapts and takes such mishaps in its jaunty hop and in its sprightly skip. So the young man alighted at the next stop having passed through a village whose name he recognised from having studied a map of Drogheda intently not twenty-four hours before. A map is scientific and abrupt and entirely unshakeable. Love is not – and when hope joins in, well, you may as well not have a map at all.

Tramping along the grass verges and the ditches and the shingle just seemed so right. As did the rain that first spattered then fell hard upon Brando as he bore on to his destination. It felt necessary to be cold. Bedraggled was the only way to be. *One day this will be in a film* he thought to himself as he bent his head against the winter gusts and balled his hands into fists just to be sure his fingers were still there. It was a cold and frozen day for sure but it was only weather after all.

For almost four hours Brando trudged on. He was Jean Valjean without the candlesticks and Long John Silver without the duplicity. He was Jack Kerouac and Tom Joad and Robinson Crusoe and Gulliver himself. Or was he just a lovelorn English fool on the rebound from a defunct marriage grasping now for green gold? Regardless, he was now deep in Drogheda searching for Hook with not a tinkerbell in sight or a moon to guide him. Yet he found it all the same. Or perhaps the village of Hook had been the one doing the searching? Let's just settle upon the fact that they met halfway – and that surely was just how it should have been.

O'Malley's Pub stood greystone and gloomy behind the sheets of rain. Though it was just midday, the low windows glowed with the light of a log-burning fire and framed in silhouette the figures of hard-drinking men. A lone chimney puffed away through the thatch of the roof and the O'Malley's sign swung in the bitter chill of the breeze like a hanged man in shock upon the gibbet. So relieved was Brando to see the pub, the first sign of life he had seen for so long, that the dreariness, the dead down beatness of the place completely passed him by. He saw the gold of the glow and not the grey of the stone.

Once inside the pub, the silence and the stillness fell upon Brando. There was an oppressiveness in the air that spoke of weariness more than wariness. Colours faded as he looked slowly about him, the only sound being the droplets of rain that fell from his sleeves onto the scarred wooden floor. None of the few drinkers that were present looked up. It was as if the door had been blown open by an errant gust and no more.

There was no sign of life behind the bar that stood but six feet from the entrance, until a short, squat man thudded from a corner table to stand behind the pumps. He beheld Brando for a not inconsiderable period of time before speaking.

"What'll it be?" he asked, the inflection in the words more suited to a statement than a question.

"Lager, please."

The barman looked at Brando as if his entire family honour had in those two words been besmirched. One or two corner-table heads turned in his direction.

"I mean, Guinness, anything. Pint of anything. Please. Anything," spluttered the flailing Englishman.

The barman nodded and slowly moved to his task, gently pulling back upon the pump lever until the glass was about half full before letting the creamy blackness whirl its swirls without interference. He gazed at the glass as the liquid settled and proceeded to dispense the rest of the pint. It was a majestic crystal ball of dark and cream and myriad scenes that had for years held many in its thrall.

"Do you have a phone I can use?" asked Brando, handing over his money for the drink.

The barman nodded towards a far corner and there Brando could vaguely discern a telephone on the wall. Taking his drink, he headed on over.

The corner was lit only by the pale winter sun that battled through the thick white sky and the cold rain. Taking the piece of paper that he had previously consulted from his pocket as a directional aid, Brando peered at it in the gloom and carefully dialled a succession of numbers. And then he waited. Just as he had chanced a mouthful of stout there came a voice at the other end of the line. Clearing his throat quickly and wiping the Guinness foam from his upper lip Brando took a breath, exhaled and spoke.

"Rosanne?"

"Yes?"

"It's me. Brando."

"Brando! I was going to call you. How was your Christmas?"

"It was okay. Not the same without you though."

There was a pause on the line before Rosanne spoke again.

"I'll be back in a couple of weeks. You know I had to come back for my family."

"I know. I didn't mean it like that. Of course. I know. It's just that I missed you. That's all."

"I've have missed you too. Strange that we've only been together a month or so," said Rosanne. "Where are you calling from?" She added. "It's very quiet."

"Oh, just a pub,"

"The Nag's Head?"

"No. It's one I've never been in before. Just came across it while I was out walking. Had to get out of the rain."

"I know what you mean. It's really been raining hard over here. Usually does though. What's it like where you are?"

"Raining. Lots of clouds. Using a payphone in the corner. I can't really see much. There are no lights on in here, just a fire which is nice. A big open fire. Hardly anybody about either."

"That does sound nice."

"And the barman was having a drink over by the door when I came in. Would never have guessed he worked here. Just up and served me then went back to his drinking."

"Sounds just like the pubs we get over here!"

Brando could almost see Rosanne's big blue eyes glisten down the phone line, providing the very means upon which her words were transported.

"It's a pretty authentic Irish pub alright," he said, trying to keep the shake from his voice.

"What's it called?" asked Rosanne in all beautiful innocence.

"O'Malley's."

"How weird! We've got an O'Malley's in Hook!"

"I know," replied Brando. "I'm in it."

EVERYTHING STOPPED.

AS IT SHOULD.

FOR JUST A WONDROUS MOMENT.

And then it all came down in the white snow avalanche that balls and rolls and destroys in spite of all that is upright and good in this world.

Ah the man he swears he's in love and he knows it to be true but it is all just a shimmer and a shudder. He has crossed the sea on a whim like only a man can. A bird, well it has reason to fly even to the other side of the world and it does that not for love but for survival, yet that is instinct also and instinct is but a shift up from what this man experiences. And he sits there on that low stool by the phone waiting for his love to appear as he sips manfully upon his stout and melds with the stony silence that is now so becoming.

You think, I guess, that the lady does not come, that she sits in her father's house, the phone still in her hand though the line is long since dead? Well it is a close thing but she does indeed arrive an hour later, her elder sister as chaperone and a look about her pretty white face that tells not of love plain and bold but of something erring towards imposition, embarrassment even. The man and the woman embrace but there is a hardness, on both sides, where once there was just a melting together. And it is only in such an embrace that a man can truly tell that he has misjudged not just the situation but his own wildly beating heart. For when love is big and true sometimes it can just come too early.

104

Brando stayed with Rosanne, at her father's house, for just one night. The rain continued on throughout and the sky was only ever shades of grey. Brando had lain awake on the sofa, the smell of burned embers upon him and the silence of stone about him. To say his heart was broken would be too much. To state that he knew no longer what love was, would be closer to the truth.

Thus did the young man fly back to his own country on New Years Eve 2010, a wife long gone and despising him and his emerald green dream just a faint swirl in the dull and impenetrable English sky.

The first few months of 2011 had been a time of reflection for Brando. He had dropped out of his post-graduate psychology course and found himself at home most days. He had neither the desire to read nor the will to dream. The few friends he had were mostly college companions who failed, despite well-meaning promises, to keep in touch. He was never to see Roseanne again, nor would anyone but her remember the romantic sojourn he had undertaken in the name of love.

So when Renbourne had offered him at last an opportunity to become an angel within the Eastern Region Angel Collective, it could not have come at a better time for Brando. He had been given the chance to be a part of something, to be above others, to bestow upon those less fortunate than he the wisdom of his experience, to offer a strong hand to the fallen. It had all seemed so right for a man for whom things had all seemed to go so wrong.

And then had come that first encounter with Liz Langford, a woman who had already fallen as far as any soul has a right to fall.

13. Beautiful Angel Of Our Times

"The Moon & Sixpence? What the fuck sort of name is that?"

Danny hadn't spoken these words in any sort of anger, for that was an emotion entirely beyond him. It was more he was just curious, that's all. Had a pupil asked him a question in class in a similar vein - *"Eric the Plumber? What the fuck sort of name is that?"* – for example, he may well have delivered some form of appropriate admonishment. Or perhaps he would have just let the moment slide with a deep down shake and an invisible grin. Actually he had been asked such a question and had indeed given the boy a detention for using foul and abusive language. But it hadn't stopped him from deep down shaking and invisibly grinning.

"It's a campsite in Suffolk," replied Alex. "I thought we might try it out. V weekend is only a couple of weeks away. Just thinking we need to get something sorted."

Danny and Ray were sitting in their usual seats at the bar and Alex was standing between them. Rod was in the non-drug toilets and Sean stood looking impassively at the closed door that led out onto New London Road wondering if opening it on this warm August day would attract custom or deter it. A brief scan of the incumbent clientele made up his mind for him.

The V Music Festival was due to take place at Highlands Park, Chelmsford on 21st August. Sean had strung up a banner outside the pub the previous year promising the finest cooked breakfast in the land and had seen little point in taking it down, despite the fraudulent nature of the culinary claim. He reasoned that hungry revellers would be grateful for anything resembling food and had been proven essentially correct in this assumption.

The local population had begun to prepare itself for an influx of strangers which involved booking weekends away, doing your weekly shop early or slumping into a resigned hurumph depending upon which way you chose to approach the particular problem of

90,000 people descending upon your provincial town, many of whom were unaware that Chelmsford was neither Glastonbury nor Cropredy.

"Up for it mate?"

"Up for what?" asked Rod as he re-appeared from round the corner.

"Camping trip. Me, Ray, Alex and you if you're up for it? Couple of days with the yokels down in Suffolk. It's about as close as you can get to going abroad these days without actually going abroad."

When you've never been a part of anything other than the combined ridicule of taller people and the morass of bad luck destined only for the out of favour, such a proposition as a camping trip with good men is liable to knock you off your little feet.

"I'll have to see what the missus thinks, but yeah, I reckon I can swing it," he replied. And it was all that he could do to remain upright.

"Sort it out then Al and let us know," said Ray. "I'll pay on my card and you scummers can pay me back before we go."

Despite not turning round Ray was as sorted inside as the rest of them. He knew more than anyone else that it is friendship that keeps you going, keeps you getting up, keeps you reeling and rocking and facing the unknowable world.

So it was that Rod, later that evening, sat in the small lounge back at his flat, Liz beside him and Jasmine lying on the floor before them both. The sun was still just visible through the bay window. The winter hum of the radiator had for some weeks now been replaced by the incessant chirping of myriad birds who thronged to the nearby park and spread out like a burgeoning city of wings. Liz turned the television up. Rod had tuned out both the birds and the voices from the screen in front of him for he had been devising a way to tell Liz about the camping trip with the lads.

"Jasmine's alright when he's like this isn't he?" he ventured. *Begin with a dog compliment*, he thought. A nice way in.

107

"How do you mean?" Liz asked between crisp-munching, not taking her eyes from the television.

"You know. Quiet. Just lying there."

"Like he was dead?" Liz turned to Rod and looked at him without one hint of emotion before resuming her gaze at whatever was being played out on the television. Her assault upon the half-price ready salted crisps continued unabated.

"How's work?" Rod tried again.

"It's just work. Same as ever," Liz replied.

So he had said something nice about the dog and asked his wife how things were at work. And, like many a man would have rightly done in the circumstances, Rod considered the groundwork to have been completed and set forth upon the task at hand.

"The lads from the pub were asking if I wanted to go away with them for a couple of days. What do you reckon?"

This time Liz didn't even look round. There was a woman on the television in tears but you couldn't hear her crying because of the music over the top. She managed a reply all the same.

"When's that then?"

Emboldened, Rod continued.

"Couple of week's time. V weekend. You're working then anyway aren't you? Just going on the Friday afternoon then back on the Monday morning I think."

Liz nodded. The music had faded out. The woman was gone. As were the tears. The adverts were back. A fat fake opera singer was selling insurance. Liz wanted to kill him. She wasn't the only one.

"So that's ok then?"

Liz nodded again. It seemed she had suddenly realised that breathing was an autonomic function. Had she tapped her leg and found it to be made of metal she would not have been at all perturbed. Her programme had finished but still she gazed at the screen. As it happened, she wasn't working V weekend. And she had told Rod that at least twice in the last couple of weeks. Not that he had listened, obviously – not that he ever seemed to listen anymore. The hardening that had begun so long ago just continued on. Anyway, now the woman on the television had stopped crying, Liz had thoughts only for Brando Anderson.

Renbourne and Eryn Rose sat opposite one another in the small kitchen of their shared accommodation. There was a sturdy, square dining room table between them and silence in the house. Brando was in his room and had been all day. Though the two angels sat across the table from one another their eye-contact was minimal. Both looked down and away whenever they could, such is the custom of angels when conversing.

"So how's Brando doing?" began Renbourne in that atonal, weary voice of his.

Eryn Rose pondered the question for a moment before answering. And that was all the response that Renbourne required. He spoke again just as she was about to respond.

"If things aren't working out then you must tell me. You do know that don't you? I must confess that I have my reservations even at this early stage. I just worry that by not bringing him into the Eastern Region Angel Collective, particularly with how things have been with him, that it may do irreparable harm to our relationship."

Eryn Rose nodded but Renbourne was looking at the linoleum floor and did not see the gentle movement of the pretty angel's head.

"There's nothing particular I can put my finger on," began Eryn Rose. "But you are right; I do have an uneasy feeling about this whole case. And I don't think it's with my man, Rod. I really believe he'll be okay. It's his wife that concerns me. I know I've only seen her once but, well, it's just a sense I get. That's all."

"Things will work out as they should," murmured Renbourne. "They always do."

"But what if they don't?"

"They always do, Eryn Rose. Sometimes things don't work out as we wish them to. That doesn't mean they don't work out as they should."

Eryn Rose, beautiful angel of our times, knew that Renbourne was right. She just didn't want him to be. So she sighed an angel sigh, stood up and leaned across the table. She placed a hand gently upon the top of Renbourne's bowed head and ruffled his short grey black hair.

"I love everybody," she said. "I can't help it. I love them all. Just like mum did."

Renbourne looked up and held both Eryn Rose's hands in his.

"That is what makes you an angel, my dear," he said as a father to a daughter, an ocean to a stream, a breath to a gasp. "That's what makes you an angel.

At 6.15 pm that same evening, Thursday August 5th 2011, police marksmen surrounded a minicab in the back of which was a man named Mark Duggan. The cab was travelling along the Ferry Lane Bridge near Tottenham Hale Station in North London. Mark Duggan was twenty-nine years old when a police officer opened fire and shot him dead in the back of the taxi. A protest march was held the following day. The march was peaceful and dignified. And there followed, in the ensuing days, what would come to be called The London Riots.

During the disturbances that took place in London between Friday 6th August 2011 and Tuesday 10th August 2011, over three thousand crimes were committed, five people were killed and sixteen were injured. It is estimated that in the region of two hundred million pounds worth of property was damaged. By early September 2011 over a thousand people had appeared in court in connection with the rioting. Two teenagers were found guilty of putting messages on the internet inciting people to riot in Northwich and Warrington. Nobody rioted in either place. The teenagers were sentenced to four years apiece in a Young Offenders Institution.

And in Chelmsford, Essex, thirty miles from where Mark Duggan had been killed, Liz Langford sat in the staff room at Wilkos a few days later staring at the television in front of her. It was the third night of rioting. It was Liz's fourth night shift in a row and it was only just past midnight. Usually by that stage she would be struggling to keep her eyes open, fighting the weariness that ever seemed to assail her. But not that night.

The small portable TV screen blazed red and orange and wailed and shook and thudded. Figures scurried in the white heat of it all, scampering into the side-streets and the alleyways, breaking apart then coming together to face the malleable rows of quaking policemen. Mobile phones were held aloft like the niggardly flagsticks of a hurt and broken system. Journalists ducked down low and tapped away on their laptops or breathed deep in ecstasy into the same devices that were being toted by the rioters. And you got to thinking that what separated one group from another was merely what they were wearing, where they were and where they were going back to. The sky was black even amidst the flames, darkened by fear and thrills and a primeval wonder that only anarchy can bring. The only truism is that lawless acts will follow lawless acts – regardless of what side you're on.

Eryn Rose lay upon her bed looking at the ceiling through red eyes, unable to gaze any further at the desecration of her Sunday, the ruination of her capital city. Her face was streaked with tears.

Sometimes it seems there are just not enough angels.

But Liz Langford's eyes, well they blazed on long after the true fires of London had been doused, blazed on into the Chelmsford night, the dry sticks of her soul having finally been brought to a spark by the very same events that brought forth tears from a distraught and impotent angel.

LOGIN - ROD
PASSWORD *******
FILE
OPEN "WIDEAWAKE"

You should have seen it! I should have been there. Coppers all over the place scared and running. Not seen anything like it ever! Shops were being looted and then going up in flames and cameramen couldn't get enough of it with their mobiles and their, you know, cameras. Not being one for telly, it's the first time that I've sat down to watch anything for more than five minutes. If it was a film it would have won all sorts of Oscars and stuff. But it wasn't, it was real and it was pretty much just down the road in London. You could see the helicopters and they were talking about bringing the army in.

Part of me wanted to get on a train and join in or maybe see if anything was kicking off in town. Couldn't though. Not right getting myself nicked when I'd promised the lads I'd go away with them. Wouldn't want to let them down – especially just to be part of some amateur tear-up.

Can't believe how easy Liz rolled over. I guess since my prison days she's had more respect for me maybe – man of the house and all that. I even got chatted up the other day – not that I told Liz about it. Don't want to break her heart or nothing like that. This bird was alright though. Called herself an angel – going a bit far with that but she's kind of desperate to see me again. Didn't say no because I didn't want to let her down you know. Must have taken a lot to approach me and stuff.

Now I've got my mates and the wife in check and suddenly killing someone seems to have taken a bit of a backseat. Got my whole

112

life though to end someone else's. No sense in rushing it. I'm not one of those knobs nicking stereos in Croydon or smacking coppers in Tottenham. You might as well just arrest yourself, find yourself guilty and lock yourself in your room.

I've just got too much about me these days. Life even feels worth living. I haven't felt that way since I was about four years old. Strange how it works.

Seeing that bird tomorrow down in Highlands Park. Don't know what to expect but might as well turn up. I'm chivalrous, me, like those Knights of the Round Table – honourable. You don't let a lady down unless you can really help it. Liz is fine with me going away with the lads so meeting this bird in the park, well, that's even more innocent. That's just a chat.

Me and the lads are going to Suffolk. That's like a different country according to Danny and he should know. He's a teacher and stuff. Only the other day he was telling me that Henry the Eighth had a brother called Eric who was a plumber. There's not many people know that sort of stuff.

SAVE

14. The Fabulous Thumpings Of This Deep Earth

Though she had been an angel for over fifteen years, Eryn Rose had only been given the opportunity to practice as an angel, in the way set out by the rules of the Eastern Region Angel Collective, on a handful of occasions. The vast majority of her angel work was done on an informal basis, during her daily wanderings and her nightly dream thinkings. Thus it was that she made sure to document the sessions she had with Rod the moment she returned home and to post them to him as soon as she was able.

Session 1 – 10th August 2011
Venue – beneath that big willow tree in Highlands Park

Rod I am so glad you came. I knew you would! You see how already I have faith in you?!

When I saw you walking up that hill, first your hair then your head then the rest of you I put my arms around the trunk of that tree (well as far as I could reach anyway!) and thanked it from the depths of my angel heart. It was like you had emerged, spirit-like, from a fog! Oh it was so wonderful to see you!!

I asked my one question –

"What brought you here today?"

You, of course said "my legs" which reminded me that I must see about getting that question revised! Of course I meant: "Tell me everything that has led you to be sitting with me beneath this magnificent tree under the grand sky of our country that is, and forever will be, Albion to me." (That is what we all have to say. It's on a card but I have memorised it!)

And all the rest was you...

I know you found it hard to talk to start with, what with just having met me and me being an angel and that, but that's where the willow tree comes in. Willow trees really are the finest listeners. They are silent when they need to be and they bend their branches just at the right moment. And you'll never make them cry in front of you – not even a single slow tear. The weeping thing is nonsense. It was just a rumour the Dutch Elms put about when they had that difficult time in the mid-seventies. Cruel really. There were a lot of problems during that time and trees really should stick together more than most.

So you were an only child, Rod. Just like me – until my brother was born anyway. When you spoke about how idyllic your life was before going to school I could really identify with that. Not in a nodding counsellor kind of way but in a 'yes that was the best time of my life as well' kind of way. And there's me ending up being an angel! But those first few years, as you describe yours, are entirely incomparable purely because at that stage we have nothing to compare them to. As a young child we have no concept of the passing of time. Clocks are the downfall of us all. That's what my dad says. Mum, when she was around, used to say it was just his excuse for being late for everything.

I won't repeat back to you all that you said to me but I will tell you what effect you had on me. I wanted to be there at the times in your life when you've been ignored, abused, misused, strung-out, hung-out, lonely and worse. I regret every single second that I wasn't there for you. But you've done alright without me – you must have done because there you were sitting just the other side of that wonderful tree telling me all these things. The regret is mine to deal with. You, Rod Langford, are a marvel.

None of us in life, not even angels, get too many compliments, not real compliments where people have tears in their eyes when they're saying them and are shaking as the words leave their mouths. It seems that as people it doesn't come naturally for us to praise each other. Yes we can bicker and snipe and gossip and gripe but mostly we can't even summon a smile for a perfect stranger.

115

So now we come to the part where you have to do some things for me, for yourself, some tasks of sorts. Here's your first two:

1. When you're walking down the street I want you to say "GOOD MORNING," to whoever you pass. Obviously say "GOOD AFTERNOON" if it's the afternoon – people will think you're mad anyway but at least you can get the time right.

2. When you've said your greeting I want you to notice the reaction of the other person and I want you to notice how you feel once you've said your words and the person has gone.

In the next two sessions I will be asking you only one question. A simple question that you will not be able to answer. And then, in time, you will be able to answer it and you won't be able to stop answering it. Then you will be happier than you've ever been before.

Remember – all that I say is true and all that I say is meant – angels know no other way…

(That last bit is just the way we end all our messages!)

Session 2 – 14<u>th</u> August 2011
Venue – beneath that big willow tree in Highlands Park

Again you came!!

I know you found last time really hard and, to be honest, it wouldn't have surprised me at all if you hadn't showed. That doesn't mean I lost my faith in you, by the way! It's just we hardly know each other, yet I expected you to tell me everything about you. People like me somehow expect a complete stranger to tell us everything about them, their lives, their fears and their worries. And do you know why people do? Do you know why you did?

a) You needed to

b) This tree gives you no choice

c) I'm pretty good at all this!

So to the question I asked you. I knew it would fool you! It does everybody! Here it is again, not that you need reminding…

"Can you tell me what's better since the last time I saw you?"

116

And your answer, again like everybody else's...

"Nothing."

Actually I think it was more like "naink." But that could have been the breeze playing with the branches and trying to fool us. It does that sometimes.

But eventually you started to talk about your tasks, the ones I set you. So you said "GOOD MORNING" to a few people! That is, as you found out, about the most wonderful way to spend your time. Yes, most of them ignored you, keeping their heads down as you described (like you used to do!) and one or two sadly responded by saying things to you that weren't very pleasant. But that elderly lady you told me about, the one you've seen around that either looks sad or scared, didn't she just light up like a roman candle whizz bang rocket flash? Imagine how she felt the rest of the day! Just think what you saying so simple a thing as "GOOD MORNING" really meant to her.

I'll tell you what it meant, Rod. It meant that this world is not as frightening as it appears, that there are good people still and that a heart, no matter how old, can still beat fast for the right reasons. You made her day, Rod. I just know it.

And who knows, perhaps she got up the following morning and changed the world. That's how this all works. That's what it leads to. It's about changing the world. That's all. And it starts with saying "GOOD MORNING" to a complete stranger.

Step one is done. Doesn't it feel so good?

So now your next tasks are:

1. Take your time with everything you do – whether it's the washing up, having a drink, smoking a cigarette or even just opening your eyes in the morning.

2. Notice every sound, every caress, every light and every shade. Be entirely alert to it all. Think where it all came from – the plate, the glass, the beer, the water even. Look deep into its journey and breathe slowly while you do it.

Just two more sessions after this. One real one and one where we say goodbye. So make the most of it!

117

Remember – all that I say is true and all that I say is meant – angels know no other way...

Session 3 – 17<u>th</u> August 2011
Venue – beneath that big willow tree in Highlands Park

It's tough, Rod, isn't it when you realise you haven't been alive since the moment you were born? Not really alive I mean. Sure you've inhaled and you've exhaled, you've put one foot in front of the other and you've closed your eyes to bring on sleep. But that's not what we're talking about is it? Not now.

You did make me laugh when you said you'd never washed anything up before! Not ever!! And you even managed, your first time, to do it with your eyes closed. That is the only way. It takes time. All this takes time. But you heard some sounds you'd never heard before – the ting and the schloosh and the sooooze and the aaaaarh. They are the most gorgeous sounds aren't they? And just while washing up! Just by closing your eyes! Just by listening! Those dishwasher machines must really be the happiest machines on this planet!!

And you see now that everything comes from within the heart and the soul and the mind of another and that nothing can be created that is not of this earth? People all around this country, this world, who you may never meet, have brought to you all that is yours – the paint on your walls, the wood of your floor, the softness in your pillow – people with lives of ups and downs and hurts and beauty and tragedy and moments where nothing is worthwhile. Yet they have brought these things to you, Rod. To you.

From the factories and the offices, the production lines, the fields and the seas comes your furniture, your newspaper, your computer, your spices and your food. And it is this earth that makes it happen. Our willow tree knows it (it's ours now by the way!) and I know it. You too now are in on the secret. Isn't it wonderful? Will things ever be quite the same again???

Of course they will be. We are people after all. It comes naturally to us to break things, to doubt ourselves, to inhibit our dreams and prohibit our visions. That's just what we're like. But remember back in that first session, when you said how you used to be when you were really young, before school even? You didn't inhibit your dreams then did you? You didn't prohibit your visions? And that was surely the happiest time of your life. Up to now.

Now let it all fall away, this grey and greasy adult skin. Take a step and a jump and before you know it you will be in that sandpit again rummaging around for your buried treasure. And you've got a park right near where you live with the greatest swing ever in it! How lucky are you???

So your final tasks are:

1. Get on that swing, push yourself off and swing high and swing low, eyes open and eyes closed and I don't want you to get off until you understand that you are magnificent.

2. Bring me a white rose. (Nothing magic in that. I just like white roses.)

One last meeting now, Rod. How quickly this has all gone!

Remember – all that I say is true and all that I say is meant – angels know no other way...

The trunks, the roots and the branches of trees are the skeleton frames that keep this entire world turning. From the oxygen leaves to the furrowed brow bark, from the juice of the sap to the crevices and hollows. Now we're not talking tree-hugging here or whatever the local media newshound fool with his camera and his ambition would like to buzzword snippety snap into his farcical article.

Whilst there is growth on this earth none of us is ever alone. Look at the lines and the angles and the flecks and the specks of all that comes from the ground. And behold for they are ONE with this us. Each time we step from our front door we are entering a one time universal garden that was once set out before us like a vast picnic blanket of wonder. So yeah there is concrete and car parks and rust

119

and oil and mayhem and shudder – but don't let that rule you. Don't let that fool you. Get on a bus, take a walk. Be drawn by the salt of the marshes and the fresh air breezes that the moon and the ocean waves do provide. Don't allow yourself to drown amidst the machinery and the acrid carve of the daily grind and the fractured, fragmented shatterings which each doleful day does bring.

Ah my heart beats with the fabulous thumpings of this deep earth. It is all vibrant ecstasy to me!

Oh and there's a bird, you know, a bird that nobody sees. But more of that later.

15. THAR BE MONSTERS

The Orwell Bridge spans the River Orwell between Wherstead and just south of Ipswich. It is almost a mile long and twenty-four metres wide. It has long been associated in times past with people jumping from it to their death. It has even been said that a number of workers died during the period of its construction in the late seventies and early eighties. For the lads in the rather weighed down Vectra though the only thing symbolised by the Orwell Bridge was that they were no longer in Essex, but in the neighbouring county of Suffolk.

England is a wonderful patchwork of counties, delineated by hedges and long-trodden paths and ranges of hills that have ever borne witness to the diminishing of the forests and the spewing of concrete upon that which was once a vast swathe of natural glory. The same could be said of any country perhaps, and justifiably so. But we're not talking here of any other country. For this is England, my England.

"Are we nearly there Ray?" asked Danny from the back seat.

"What are you, five?" Ray replied, keeping his eyes firmly on the road, not wanting to miss the exit off the A12 dual carriageway that would take them to within ten minutes of the campsite.

Danny smiled, raised his eyebrows at Rod who sat beside him, and finished off his second can of lager of the morning. Rod smiled back up at his friend and felt at that moment he was flying in the air as opposed to just coming to the end of the Orwell Bridge. Just leaving the environs of Chelmsford, the confines of the flat, the walls of the prison and the receding tentacles of probation was like having grown a foot taller.

Rod had packed the previous night with the enthusiasm of a child going on his first school trip. Liz had eyed him without comment, noticing how he seemed to be trying to slow himself down when it was quite clear he just couldn't wait to get away. She bore this knowledge not with malice but merely with acceptance. The man who professed to love her was evidently more enamoured of spending time with his new friends than with his own wife.

Ray, despite all distractions, took the correct slip road and soon the concrete and fumes that had characterised their journey thus far were replaced with silence and the country green shades of a different time, a palette long discarded by those who commit us to a life of hard edges and the straight lines of progress in the name of government and devolved power.

What once was, will always sustain. What has ever been, ever will be. The heart of a people is in its soil, not in its temporary ministers or its transient media. They are but mere distractions akin to having a five year old man with a beard in the back of your car, whilst a midget looks upon him admiringly, giggling at his every, admittedly funny, remark.

As midday approached, the lads arrived at The Moon & Sixpence campsite. Ray had negotiated the twists and turns of the country lanes relying on his innate sense of direction. The satellite navigation device he had received the previous Christmas had been of little help once he had left the ravages of the 21st century. The message 'THAR BE MONSTERS' was all it could manage before switching itself off in a puritanical sulk.

The entrance to the campsite was set back off the road around a sharp left hand bend and the first Ray was aware that he had missed it was when he felt a nudge from Alex's elbow.

"Just passed it, mate, I think. Back there a touch."

"Bollocks," muttered Ray as he drove on to the next turning, the country road having narrowed to more or less one lane making a U-turn not just dangerous but virtually impossible. The encouragement from the backseat, although well intended had done nothing to widen the road or straighten the bend. There had been times during the journey during which Ray had felt like a taxi-driver. At other times he had felt like a father. But mostly he had just felt like a good friend. And he rightly knew of no finer sensation. So a frantic U-turn later and they had arrived at their destination.

On either side as they drove into the site were two large signposts – yellow lettering on a royal blue background. Each sign bore the words 'Moon & Sixpence', arching over a smiling golden half-moon. The wide tarmac drive was flanked by neatly cut grass and a rickety wooden fence constructed of wayward saplings wound round chunky posts that had been thumped into the ground. The horizon was adorned with broad splashes of ash trees, oak and birch, the deep wide sky between them seeming to throb as the breeze eased through the upper branches of the trees. Beyond the entrance the tarmac road fed round to the right between luxurious static caravans and dipped down to the left where the booking-in chalet was situated.

Ray pulled the Vectra into the car park a little way down the hill, got out of the car and walked the short distance to check in. He confirmed the necessary details with the woman behind the reception desk and glanced through a caravan brochure on the counter whilst she wrote his details in a large ledger using a blue betting shop pen. He went back to the car to find his passengers all still in situ, awaiting his return.

Danny and Rod exited the car by their respective doors and Alex was the last out. Still, he was the first to open the boot and the first to begin to unload the bags and the tent.

The lads stood in silence for a moment, standing by the car smoking and looking around, surveying the scene as they inhaled and exhaled the nicotine. An old couple walked up the hill towards them, nodded in their direction and carried on up and around the bend in the direction of the large static caravans. Despite his leather jacket feeling hot and heavy upon him on that mid-summer day, Rod had never felt cooler in his life. Here he was, with his mates, out in the great wide open.

When you're so small, to feel so cool is something to which you can only ever dream to aspire. The steeple, people, can only be hewn from the quarry of our disparate desperations by those who we are honoured to call our mates. And that's the truth of it, the deep down honest truth of what keeps a man going in these hard, hard times. Just surround yourself with good people and live as simply as you can.

"What now then Ray?" asked Alex, bags at this feet and boot clicked   shut.

The car indicators winked smugly in response to Ray having set the alarm and a warm breeze swept up the hill, twirling briefly around the legs of the four men before dissipating with a gentle sigh upon the burgeoning tarmacadam rise.

"Down this slope about two hundred yards and our pitch is opposite the lake, right at the back."

The lads picked up their bags and Alex, who had just a holdall over his shoulder, carried the packaged tent.

"We'll get sorted then come back for the booze," added Ray.

The heat that rose from the engine through the bonnet of the car created a shimmering haze that could have been mistaken for a deep breath. It would take at least a couple of trips to ferry the alcohol from the boot to the tent. There was a lot of it. And rightly so.

The man-made lake at The Moon & Sixpence was at the foot of the hill. It was fronted at the road end by a sandy expanse which was rather grandly referred to as 'the beach', with the other three sides hemmed in by overhanging grass banks which were themselves bordered by trees and shrubs. In the centre of the lake was an isle which contained densely packed shrubs and small trees, a haven for the ducks and other wildlife who called this artifice their home. There was no landing point for curious children, no matter how hard the occasional determined scamp may try to claim the isle as his own. The depths at the far end of the lake seemed almost incalculable and added a cool majesty to what was in essence just a hole filled with water. But the reeds had grown around the edges over time and the birds and the insects had settled in, lending a natural splendour to all things.

So before long it wasn't the lake that smacked of artifice but the fragile tents and the static caravans that were magnets for the roving souls and the retired couples who still strived, after all these years, to find a simpler way to be. And may those souls one day stop roving and may their striving not be in vain.

The pitch was, as Ray had described – about as far back from the lake as you could be, tucked away in the corner of the tent part of the site, a corner comprising of a brambly hedge going west and an equally unfriendly ditch leading north. Beyond the ditch was a fallow field and on the other side of the hedge was the recreational part of the site.

The Moon & Sixpence was busy and buzzing with the summertime dreamy doings of errant children and the back to basics nature ways of their parents. As the four men walked through the rows of guy-ropes and tents and awnings and chairs and plastic tables and attempts at refinement and men dreaming of a pint in the clubhouse up the top, they sensed that this was going to be a particular sort of weekend.

"Fuck me," remarked Danny. "Not exactly the Playboy mansion is it?"

Alex smiled and chuckled silently in the way that only wise people can. Mountains chuckle too if you wait long enough and get up really close. And you've all heard streams giggle, surely, as the reeds shush them and the wild mountain thyme whispers sweet to the boldly blooming heather? I will go, lassie. I will surely go.

"Danny, mate," said Ray, throwing his bag on the ground in the manner of Shackleton planting his flag, "you squint hard enough, drink hard enough and wank hard enough and this place can be paradise for you. Now stop being a big girl and give us a hand to get this tent up. The quicker we do that the quicker we can have a drink."

And there was no way that any of them could follow that.

The time had come then to erect the Vango Oregon 600. Danny unzipped the bag containing the tent and briefly glanced at the

125

instruction sheet before stuffing it into the back pocket of his jeans. It looked far too much like a lesson plan for his liking. He then proceeded, with Rod's help, to empty the bag – canvases, colour-coded poles, guy ropes, pegs – the lot. What lay before him did not seem to Danny very close to a structure that would house the four of them for the weekend. Undeterred, he felt for the instruction leaflet and found that it was no longer in the pocket to which he had dismissed it just moments ago. Ray had retrieved it as Danny had been intent upon the decanting of the bag and he and Alex were at that point kneeling down studying the diagrams.

"Give us a hand with the beer Rod," said Danny. "Any luck we might have a tent to come back to. Chuck us the keys, Ray."

Ray threw the car keys in Danny's general direction without looking up from the leaflet. Rod shot up a hand, caught the keys beautifully and strolled up the hill to the car with his mate. The sun rose higher. The lake glistened and, taking heart from the newcomers, one or two dads snapped open a sneaky can.

"At this time of day?"

"Yes love. We're on holiday, remember?"

And the wives shake their heads and wonder at the enormity that is their approaching middle years. A chance enquiry from a now emboldened husband as to whether a quick blowjob is out of the question whilst the kids are playing up on the rope-swing falls sadly on unromantic ground.

Ah and my England rolls on.

So as the hordes descended upon Chelmsford on Friday 21st August 2011 to join those who had already arrived at Highlands Park to attend the V music festival, four friends were at an idyllic campsite in the next county – two schoolteachers, an arborist and a midget who had yet to acknowledge that it had been at least a week since he had thought about killing anybody. But more importantly, as it was to turn out, he had left himself logged-on to the computer in the flat he shared with his slightly taller wife who most certainly had plans of her own.

16. Producing A Hat From A Rabbit

An adult human skeleton consists of two hundred and six bones. The hands and feet account for one hundred and six and the head (including six ear bones!) includes another twenty-eight. There are twenty-five bones in the chest, twenty-six in the back and the remainder are split, in minimal numbers, amongst the throat, shoulders, arms, legs and pelvis.

Bones are broken and repaired, they slip out of place and then back in, held together largely by muscles and ligaments with some tissue filling the gaps. In addition, we have forty-three pairs of nerves, twelve of which go back and forth from the brain and the other thirty-one emanating from the spinal chord with a combined length of forty-five miles. Yes, forty five miles of nerves buzzing throughout one human body. But that is as nothing compared to the circulatory system which is, wait for it, sixty thousand miles in length. That's more than twice the circumference of this baffling earth.

Yet there are people who are intent on ending all that wonder, blistering it into nothing, whether it be their job or their moral stance or their righteousness or their voice of God. To kill another is as easy as plucking the petals from a flower or snipping its stem, taking an axe to a tree or choking the ocean with your oil spills and all that industrial excrement you call progress. Heroes don't kill. Killing doesn't make you a hero. All you've done is taken the head off a dandelion. And what's heroic about that?

For so many years we look for perfection, seek miracles and implore the world to show us its beauty. We pay thousands to witness the rumble crash of Niagara Falls, the lonesome orange deepdowns of The Grand Canyon or the pungent green swelterings of the rain forests. But just look in the mirror at yourself. That is the true miracle. And every single tiny motion you make is a miracle too. Think of those veins a-pumping and those nerves a-humming and the incomprehensible unknowing entity that is your mind.

But it's all very well for me. I'm just sitting on the floor of my discarded clothes, empty beer-canned bedroom. I don't work night after night in doleful silence in a large supermarket, taking early shifts when I can get them just to feel more human. And the person I'm married to hasn't just left me lonesome to spend a weekend with three men that he didn't even know until six weeks ago. I'm not Elizabeth Langford. That's true.

When Liz had met Brando that first time, she had left Trinity Park with a flickering glimmer within her. She had been so resigned in her life to the narrow, stale wanderings of her thoughts and the dull thud of her laden heart that anything remotely different, such as being followed home by a not unattractive man, was bound to awaken something within her. So at their second meeting, again in Trinity Park, on a bench by the playground, she was a little more prepared than had previously been the case.

"Hello," said Brando, as Liz approached. He felt that he may have spoken a little too early and wasn't sure if she had heard him. She had the countenance of one who was hard of hearing or perhaps just someone who had given up listening. Whatever it was, her face remained impassive as she sat down beside him. She looked at the slide and the climbing frame with an intensity that made Brando wonder if it was her gaze alone that kept everything standing.

After a minute or so she spoke in a flat, barely audible voice.

"Rod's gone away this morning," she said. "With his new friends."

Brando already knew. Eryn Rose, having gone looking for Rod in The Setting Sun when he hadn't turned up for his final session with her, had been met by a grim-faced Sean. "He's gone camping with the other idiots. And you should wear something on your feet next time you come in here." Eryn had departed gracefully if a little perturbed. Sean had been left to his empty pub, cursing the day his washing machine had been stolen. He'd been sullenly withdrawn from the illicit drug chain since then and given the fact that it was the Friday of V weekend, he began to regret how things had transpired. And vengeance grew within him. His knives blinked in his direction like a pair of lighthouses whilst the darts did all they could to instil life into their plastic flights in order to finally make a break for it.

"Ok," replied Brando. "So how do you feel about that?"

Liz turned to face him and he appeared to shrink back a little. She ignored his question entirely.

"So why did you want to see me? Can you tell me again?"

Brando knew he had to choose his words with care. The moment felt precarious, crucial even.

"It's hard to explain," he began. "You see I have to be honest, am told to be honest. I am honest."

A word or two from Liz would have been helpful to him, a nod maybe – just some encouragement to make the would-be angel feel that at least his tone was right, even if the words were somewhat awkward. But there was nothing, no acknowledgement at all that he was even speaking a language that was familiar to her.

The small grey birds that gave flesh to the dry twigs and cracked branches of the nearby trees withdrew a little. There are no more instinctive beings than birds. They have more freedom than a mere human can even imagine yet they still deign to be amongst us. Pigeons will scrabble on the ground for morsels; seagulls will swoop down and demean themselves by snatching that buttered bread from your very fingers. Think of these events as an interaction only. And feel honoured that your concrete is so noble and your sandwich so delightful that these wonderful, incredible beings are even remotely interested. There's a hierarchy for sure my friends and it is top down – believe me.

The word 'honest' meant nothing to Liz, even when it came from the mouth of a man who was giving her more attention than she had known for a long old time. To understand such a concept as honesty it helps perhaps to be cognisant of what it is to fall foul of dishonesty or to have been confronted with cold hard lies. The concept of honesty, even the word itself, can become for some just a combination of letters as opposed to a way of being. For Liz, the word 'honest' belonged in the same category as words like 'hope' and 'wonder' as far as she was concerned. Meaningless – all of them.

"Well, basically," continued Brando, undeterred though most definitely daunted, "there are people I am connected with who are concerned about your husband. They can see him potentially getting himself in some sort of trouble but at the same time they believe him to be a good person. I'm here to support you and to see if there is any advice you can give us to make sure that Rod, your husband, is going to be, well, safe."

"He's gone away," replied Liz.

She hadn't even paused to think. Her words were mere facts with no vestige of emotion. She had heard Brando, processed the information in a way only she could, and replied. Interaction over.

"I appreciate that," persisted Brando. She was giving him nothing to work with, it was clear. "When will he be back?"

"Monday morning."

"That's not far away. What are his friends like?"

"They buy him drinks and he buys them drinks and he's in the pub with them all the time. I know them to look at. One of them spoke to me once."

Again, just facts. No distress. No heartache. Not even close.

"So are they a good influence do you think? I mean could it be that now he's hanging around with them that he will be ok, like, you know, start getting things back on track – after prison and probation? Back to how he once was?"

"How old are you?" Liz asked, the pitch of her voice raised a little from the previous dull monotone. It was like she'd had just a tiny intake of helium.

It was then that Brando became aware that she had been moving imperceptibly closer to him along the bench. Or perhaps it had been he that had been inching unknowingly towards her?

However it had happened, what was clear was that her thigh was touching his. What was equally clear to Brando was that his limbs felt too heavy to even move. So there they stayed, Liz staring into the empty playground and Brando, pale and motionless.

"Twenty-nine," he replied.

The beating of his heart was unrelenting. Even the trees behind the incongruous couple withdrew slightly, not quite appalled, but most definitely unsettled.

That same Friday afternoon, some forty-nine miles away, Rod Langford was far from unsettled. He and Danny were lying on the grass outside their tent drinking beer and looking up at the sky. Sure, both had experienced that feeling of not quite getting it right with the odd dribble of alcohol escaping the can as they poured it into their open mouths, the golden liquid trickling down the side of the face, around the ear and through the hair to escape into the grass. But such an act as the one in which they were so blissfully engaged was worth a sticky cheek. You're fine supine on the grass and you're looking up into the grand English sky. Oh yeah.

"If you close your eyes, mate, and pretend it's someone else tipping the can it's like you're a Roman Emperor being fed grapes or something by some gorgeous topless wench," stated Danny, in-between gulps.

Rod closed his eyes. Danny was right – no doubt about it.

"If you were a Roman Emperor," asked Rod, "what would you call yourself?"

"Eric," replied Danny without hesitation.

"Like the plumber?"

"Rod mate. You are priceless. Genuinely priceless."

So it was that Alex and Ray arrived back at the tent, laden down with carrier bags of supplies from the supermarket in the local village to find their two friends stretched out on the floor, eyes closed to the day and entirely lost in their own sumptuous reveries as the beer tumbled from the cans they held aloft, cascading into their open mouths like the most beautiful of waterfalls. And more wonderful still was that Ray and Alex did not disturb them. They got along with decanting the bags into one of the spare compartments in the tent the two of them had erected.

That evening bore witness to one of the truly fundamental experiences a person can have – the preparing and cooking of food outdoors for the edification and yumness of good people. The gentle pinkish skittings of the sky just above the trees that isolated the campsite from the wider world, the thring-throng sing-song of tiny birds and the sparkle shimmer of the lake's water were all suddenly wrought upon the consciousness - eyes, ears and all senses heightened to their ultimate delight by the sheer gorgeousness of what was being heated, stirred, turned and moved by spatulas and long forks and brave hands. Ah there is nothing like it.

MAN I AM FLYING!

Alex had set up two identical round-bottomed turquoise camping stoves on the dry grass to the left of the tent entrance. He had a large frying pan heating up upon one and a saucepan upon the other in which a curry made from tinned tomatoes, chopped onions, chicken, chopped coriander, cumin, turmeric, chillies, potatoes, garlic and butter was simmering away, puffing mystical eastern fragrance and vaporous devilment into the summer evening air. And magical is the word – the transformation of the products of the earth that emerge from the bubbling pot of witchy legend - oh there is NOTHING more magical than that, not sawing a woman in half, pulling flowers from your sleeve or producing a hat from a rabbit.

Just inside the tent, Ray was mixing flour, water, salt, pepper and ground coriander until he had a small wad of dough. Taking off a thumb-size piece and fashioning a ball between his palms he rolled it out onto the big round wooden chopping board his wife had forbidden him to take from the kitchen at home. When he had a thin, almost translucent disc, he handed the board to Danny who slid the disc into the boiling oil that had by now begun to pop and fizzle in the frying pan. And moments later after more magic, a naanadon was born – a hybrid of poppadum and naan bread. Rod slipped a metal spatula underneath the naanadon and gently placed it on a waiting plate that Alex held in his hands. They repeated this process until six naanadons had been wrought from the dough.

Before long the curry was ready, the rice that had been prepared earlier was unveiled from beneath the damp tea-towel that had been taking care of it and the naanadons were piled high. There was beer and cider for now and whisky for later. The sun was sinking and the moon was on the rise. The stars were backstage, all nativity play excited and the sky itself just had to let it all unfold. The lake was dark. The fish were asleep. And the ducks had nestled into themselves on the isle in the centre upon which no man had stood since its very creation.

The evening was passed in deep talk, mad talk, ridicule, reminiscence and whisky from the bottle. During it all, the ties that bind one person to another were bound just that little bit more tightly.

As the lads at The Moon & Sixpence at last retreated to the safety of their tent, zipping themselves first into their individual compartments and then into their sleeping bags, Liz Langford wheeled a trolley full of wine bottles over to the alcohol section that had been depleted by the first wave of music fans who were just getting into the groove a mile down the road in Highlands Park. She mechanically picked up each bottle, sliding them one at a time onto the shelves. Her round face reflected grotesquely in the neck and shoulders of the dark glass, twisted, elongated and deformed. In former times she perhaps would have averted her eyes at the disfigurement. Now though, at just approaching one o'clock in the morning, she could barely supress a smile. In fact, if you had been standing behind her you may have seen her shoulders rising and falling in a manner consistent with unrestrained giggling. Yet not a sound left her red raw lips.

134

17. Buddha Barmish Man Of Peace

"It started with a piss - I never thought it would come to this..." sang Danny as he urinated into the hedge some twenty yards behind the tent. He had been the last to rise, stirred from his sleep no doubt by the sputtering of sausages, the fizzletish of bacon and the gentle popping of eggs. Ray had masterfully brought all the elements of the most marvellous of breakfasts to a climax in the large frying pan. Alex was responsible for the delectable waft of morning coffee and Rod had sorted out the plates, cutlery, bread and sauces.

"Looks like you're washing up then, Dan," said Ray as his mate sauntered back to join the others. Rod handed Danny a plate and they all indulged in the breakfast of kings, the breakfast of true champions. And not one of them spoke as they ate. For nobody had the capacity for words, so good was the food and so necessary the act.

It was as Danny was half-heartedly dipping the plates in a plastic bowl of soapy water (what Eryn Rose would have considered a 'washing-up opportunity') that two men approached him.

"Alright mate?" said the first. The other man held up his right hand and nodded in a beautiful time-tested gesture of peace.

Danny looked up, soapsud bubbles dripping from his forearms and his glasses a little steamed from the water. Ray emerged from the tent, where he had just finished shaving, and greeted the men on behalf of his clan.

"Morning," he said, fully expecting a complaint about the well into the early hours conversations that had been had or the flagrant disregard for the local shrubbery that had been displayed by one of his group. He was absolutely ready to defend against all comers.

"Morning," replied the first man, paying homage to the customs of this new tribe. "Just wondered if you'd be interested in this." The man handed Ray a sheet of paper. "Let us know by eleven if you can. If we can get enough people we'll drive down and book it."

Ray nodded. "Will do," he said. "Cheers."

The two men wandered back to a large green tent some thirty yards closer to the lake. From the expression on the faces of the two women outside that tent, it seemed these particular men were perhaps in for an uncomfortable morning.

Boarders repelled, Ray took a look at the piece of paper. The writing was in large capital letters and written in fluorescent yellow pen. It must have seemed a good idea at the time, thought Ray as he held the sheet up in front of him.

"TRYING TO GET A TEAM TOGETHER FOR PAINT-BALLING ON SUNDAY 23rd. LET PAUL AND TIM KNOW IF YOU'RE INTERESTED. NEED TO GET TEN OF US IF POSS. WE'RE IN THE GREEN TENT BY THE SHOWER/WASHING CABIN."

It took very little time for Ray to convince Alex, Danny and Rod that this was something they just had to do. Even Alex's inherent pacifist nature and Danny's desire for a blissful afternoon watching the cricket in the clubhouse were no match for a lads against the world moment. And Rod? Well he just couldn't wait.

To the chagrin and plain annoyance of two palpably angry wives, Paul and Tim had sufficient takers to be able to form their paintball team. Aside from the lads, there was Geoff - a man in his fifties from Birmingham who was camping alone - and a father and son duo, both of whom had hair as orange as orange and faces as pale as could be. Both of them were called Frank.

So that was it – Paul, Tim, Geoff, Ray, Alex, Danny, Rod, Big Frank and Little Frank – going to war for four hours on the day of the Lord against the local Suffolk hordes. Just like old times for the boys of Essex. If only they could have brought with them that sturdy Russian Cannon from Trinity Park. But that was no loss really – for their secret weapon was already amongst their number, though they knew it not.

The Moon & Sixpence had originally been just a campsite, but over the years it had grown substantially. The lake had been dug and filled, populated with fish and reeds and, of course, the tiny island. The tent pitches had been squeezed on both sides by banks of static caravans and lodges and ringed by paths and walkways. And over time a sporting aspect had been developed and was evident in all its glory if you walked between the lake on the left and the tent pitches on the right, up the hill, through the trees and out into the great wide open. There were three clay tennis courts, a basketball court, a volleyball set-up complete with sand, a table-tennis table and even petanque for the more discerning and genteel.

To top it all off there was a half-size football pitch with half-size goals and a beautiful nine-hole golf course which was a little more than pitch and putt but not quite St Andrews. And just to think, thirty years earlier the finest recreation to be had around the site was wandering through the fields of golden stubble looking for expelled gun cartridges. They were mainly a pale red colour, tubular with a blackening around the edges. I should know - I found a few in my time and was exhilarated at every single find. The same as I loved the small china (probably not china!) animals they sold in the campsite shop and the Paul Daniels magic tricks and the jigsaw puzzles. But anyway, onwards!

Saturday afternoon was spent, as it should be, kicking a ball around the field interspersed with lying in the sun, talking about books and films and music and previous escapades. Danny, Ray and Rod retired back to the tent for a break from the sun whilst Alex wandered over to the lake.

The beach was cold, wet and soft under Alex's bare feet, the overhanging trees having shielded it from the mid-day sun. Children dug trenches around meticulous sandcastles and then created furrows that reached down towards the edge of the lake. They filled garish plastic buckets with water and emptied them around the sandcastles, watching the trenches fill, mesmerised by the erosion and the motion, gazing in profundity as the water made its way back via the furrows to its source. And then they just stood there in silence entranced by the lapping of the ebb and the flow, entirely enthralled by the white water wisps that skated across where the beach met the lake.

A couple, perhaps in their seventies, held hands, standing knee deep in the lake, their trouser-legs rolled up. They both looked towards the isle in the centre, seeing different things, feeling a different breeze, waiting for something unknown to the rest of us. The water around them and the sand between their toes held them solid, engaged their very beings in the shimmer and shake of this earth. It was as if they had returned in wonder to the site of their baptism to await further instruction.

What the old man should have been instructed to do at that exact moment was to move his head slightly to the left. He would then have successfully avoided the sponge ball that had been on-driven beautifully by a seven year old girl; leaving her father, the bowler, to consider the sandy wicket as being a batsman's track after all. But the old man didn't even turn round. Perhaps he hadn't even felt it, hadn't heard the ball plop down into the water behind him.

Perhaps, thought Alex, none of this was really happening. He considered this further as he walked along the right hand side of the lake to the grassy mound at the far end, away from the beach and the children, the sounds of play and the schism of generations. The dense thicket of trees on the isle shielded his view of the beach and in some way acted as a filter that sifted out any extraneous man-made sound, leaving only beauty nature arias.

Alex sat on the grass beneath the shadow of the trees behind him, the shadows that are the product of the forests of this land and the sun in the sky – the true link to our earliest days. It is an absolute truth that for as long as there has been light in the sky, there has always been a propensity for darkness to be cast upon this earth.

The conversations of birds and the schlop and schlap of the water against the grassy bank were beautiful to Alex. These wonderful sounds were interspersed on occasion by the popping bubbles of breath-taking fish taking a breath and the squeaky mwack, mwack of ill-tempered ducks. Alex crossed his legs, allowed his palms to rest gently upon his knees, closed his eyes and breathed with his entire being. And he spoke in a low voice without inflection, like the hum of the wings of the bird that nobody sees.

Forgive everybody everything
And I love you
Recognise beauty wherever it be
And I love you
Understand the nature of loss
And I love you
Give love wherever you go
And I love you
Anger devours the soul
And I love you
Look deep or don't look at all
And I love you
Imagination is life
And I love you
Trust everybody
And I love you
You are wonderful
And I love you

Over and over again he repeated this meditation, all the while concentrating only on the life he breathed in and the life he exhaled. He was a Buddha, a Bhikkhu, a Bodhisattva and he was you and he was me. He was the trunk of the tree, the stem of the flowers and the very thudding of the hearts that beat through this world. He was the ducks in the lake and the fish deep in hiding, the sponge ball, the hands held in supplication and the wisps of white that wash upon the shoreline. Yet not a shadow did he cast.

Rod left Danny and Ray dozing in the mid-afternoon sunshine and walked towards the enclosed beach. Lunchtime had brought with it a hiatus in the waterside activities and a tractor wobbled its way up the hill towards the golf course having just raked the sand, disposing of sandcastle kingdoms, transforming turning wickets and sandy furrows, bays and tributaries once more into a blank canvas.

Ducks and birds nested siesta style in the safety of the isle and even the water itself appeared to be at rest. It was just the sway swoon sway of the very tops of the trees that gave any indication of motion. Or perhaps it was the sky that was moving? Beauty and magic need no explanation and nor should one ever be sought. If I see in my mind the sky waltzing with the puff sigh clouds and the trees in static awe and the lake consisting of nothing but layers of time, then that is what I see. We are all heaven. I know that for sure.

It's not always easy to know what to do when you happen upon your friend meditating. If it wasn't for the words Alex was speaking, Rod would have considered him to have been asleep. Alex's mantra was interspersed by moments of breathing whilst all along his limbs remained entirely still, in the pose of relaxation he had adopted at the outset. That didn't mean though that he wasn't alert. The thing with meditation is that it heightens your senses. Well that's the idea, anyway.

"Freeze!"

Rod paused mid-step, his left foot hovering above the grass for just a moment before he turned and shambled over to sit beside this Buddha barmish man of peace.

"Sorry Al," he said. "Was just going for a walk. Didn't know you were here."

Alex smiled. "Nothing to be sorry for mate. Did you bring any cans with you?"

Rod shook his head. "No. Sorry."

"Ah well."

"I didn't know you were religious," said Rod.

"I'm not."

"Oh, I thought you were praying that's all."

"Just doing my meditations. I try and get in three a day. Stops me killing people." He looked at his small friend and winked.

Alex was as much into drink and music and laughs as the rest of the lads but they each had their own way of being alone.

"It sounded a bit like a song you were doing."

"Not a song. Just words."

"Do you make them up, the words?"

"Sometimes. I got the one I was just doing out of a book though," Alex replied.

"Oh right. What like a prayer book?"

Alex smiled again. In fact he smiled, to some degree, almost permanently. It would be perhaps more apposite to account for the times when he didn't smile.

"No. I copied this out from a manuscript one of my mates gave me. He's a reader for a publishing company. If there's anything he thinks I'd like and the publisher doesn't, he gives them to me. Saves on his shredding bill."

"What's it called?" asked Rod.

"The manuscript? Tollesbury something or other. By some bloke who used to drink in Chelmsford apparently. He's from round our way I think, so my mate said. I liked it. Bit mad though so I can see why it got turned down. There's a thing in it called FRUGALITY, just lines you know. That's what I was saying when you thought I was praying. I added some extra stuff to stretch it out a bit and make the breathing more rhythmic."

"How does it go?"

"Coming into the fold then, Rod? You'll have to get that hair of yours cut. Baldies only in this gang."

Now it was Rod's turn to smile. Still the sky waltzed silently with the clouds and the tree trunks provided the bar lines within which all this gorgeous music was played out.

"Seriously though mate, it's good stuff. Do you want to hear it?"

"If you like."

"I won't do all the meditating bollocks or the bits I added. Anyway, it's nine lines that in some strange way are kind of comforting – gives you hope, you know?" said Alex. "Especially when your mate comes over to you empty handed just when a can of cider would have been pure gold," he added.

Before Rod could apologise for the third time, Alex spoke to him the nine lines of FRUGALITY.

And a suitable silence followed. Even the sky and the clouds, brought to a halt by a tall tree branch finger to wood bark lips, gazed down upon the two men who sat by the edge of the lake.

"None of it rhymes," said Rod, eventually, turning to look at Alex, who was wide-eyed and expectant.

"Ah you fucker, Rod. It's not supposed to rhyme."

"Well what is it then?"

"What it says."

"Do it again. I don't get it," stated Rod. But subconsciously he understood far more than he was at that time able to acknowledge. For he hadn't realised yet that he was wonderful. That would be a long time in coming even for a man who had so recently been ministered to by an angel. But an angel can only ever take you part of the way. It's your mates that do the rest.

"Right. First," began Alex, "you have to forgive everybody everything – anyone that has ever hurt you, put you down, let you down – all that stuff. Just forgive them. You just say 'I forgive you,' and let it go. It works. Trust me. Let it go"

Rod looked at his friend, not saying a word.

"You've got to do it. I can't really help you out on this one. I don't know who's done what to you over the years, Rod, mate. I only met you a few weeks back. Just think about those people and let them go, let what they did to you go."

"What's the letting go bit?" asked Rod quietly, so quietly the trees bent their branches a little and the water in the lake rippled towards the grassy bank just to be able to hear that bit better.

"All the difficult things that have ever happened to you, have ever happened to any of us, only exist because we keep them. Just let them leave you, over your head, up through the trees and into the sky, over the clouds and to where you can't even picture. Forgiveness is the letting go. Mate you will feel so much lighter, so much, I don't know, cleaner in a way. Not that you're not clean, but, well, you kind of get rid of all that stuff that brings you down. Just let it go. Go on."

By the time Alex had finished, Rod had already forgiven everybody everything. When it came to it, he had barely been wronged by anyone and had just been unlucky on occasion – the washing machine and the drugs being fairly typical of his misfortune. It was his own responses that had actually done the damage. He had let these misfortunes persecute him over the years, bear down upon him as if they were mounds of dirt shovelled onto his already rotting carcass. All Alex did was give him a spade. And then he was clear. Daylight. Dry. Free.

"What's next?" he asked.

"You've done it?" replied a somewhat startled Alex.

"Yeah. What's next?"

"Everyone? Everything?"

"Yeah."

"Then what's next is we go back to the tent, have a drink, bit of music, some puff and maybe get Ray's guitar out."

"What about the rest of the FRUGALITY thing?"

"Mate," replied Alex," helping his friend to his feet. "If you can forgive everybody everything you're a better man than me. Now let's get going before those two bastards wake up and drink all the cider."

"Well can you write it down for me? The FRUGALITY thing?"

"Of course mate. I'll even dig out the manuscript for you when we get back if you like."

Now that's a Buddha for you.

That's a real gone Buddha.

18. We Are To Be Angels

The Eastern Region Angel Collective was established on 13th August 1984 at a bedside in Ipswich & East Suffolk Hospital where Renbourne Anderson, then twenty-five years old, visited his wife, Suzanne. Her last chemotherapy session was over. She had been diagnosed with breast cancer and had six months left to live of the nine the consultant had previously allotted her. But like many predictions, optimism was a little too much to the fore. In reality, she would be dead by Christmas, leaving behind her husband, a daughter of seven and a son of two.

When Renbourne arrived, Suzanne greeted him with the biggest, widest, most gorgeous smile you ever saw. Her eyes were brighter than any star in any sky and they had the dark depths of the entire universe within them. Renbourne's first thought was that she had been told that suddenly she was cured and the cancer was gone.

"Oh Renbourne!" Suzanne whispered after he had put his arms around her and rested his head upon her shoulder. She was sitting up in bed and would be able to leave within the hour once the doctor had done his rounds. "Oh Renbourne, I have so much to tell you!"

"Let's get you home first. You need your rest."

Suzanne did not stop smiling until she was back home, sitting on the settee just bursting to tell her husband what had taken hold of her in so wonderful a fashion. Naturally weary, often distraught and inherently sceptical, Renbourne looked at her as if he were trying to remember every detail of her beautiful face – preparing for when that terrible time came when it would exist only in photographs and darknight imagebright trauma. The doctor had mentioned nothing about the cancer abating. Actually, he had barely said a word.

"I had a dream last night, Renbourne, a vision. It was incredible. It was so real!"

"It was probably just the drugs they give you in there. You mustn't get over-excited Suzie," replied Renbourne standing before her. "It will take too much out of you."

Suzanne rose from the sofa and sat on the floor.

"Where are the children?" she asked.

"With Maria. I'll call her and tell her we're back. She said she would quite happily have them overnight though. You should get some rest."

"No. I want them to be here when I tell you what I saw, what happened."

"It's gone nine. They're probably asleep as it is."

Suzanne took a deep breath and the colour in her face waned a little. "Renbourne. Please. For me."

Renbourne called his sister and a quarter of an hour later Eryn Rose, red cheeked and wide-eyed but still awake, sat beside her mother on the floor with her head in her lap. Brando, who had been laid gently on the sofa, his two year old self oblivious to the fact he was no longer at his aunt's house slept quietly where he lay.

"Eryn Rose, lift up your head for Mummy. I've got something to tell you and Daddy.

And there they were, a husband on the verge of falling apart, a young girl who knew more then anyone could imagine and a dozing baby boy who for the remainder of his short life would ever wish that he had been at least awake during the moments that were to follow.

"I was visited in the night by what I can only describe as a bird, but it's a bird that nobody sees. I felt it beside me and around me, could feel the air move as it flapped its wings. I closed my eyes because it was useless to keep looking for something I couldn't see. And when I closed them the movements in the air were transformed into breaths and the breaths into words and that's what I need to tell you. We are to be angels, Renbourne, both of us! And in time the children will be angels too. We are to dedicate our lives to helping people that need us, people that are on the edge of falling down. Our job will be to pick them up and we'll do that by getting them to realise that their life is precious and that the world is wonderful!"

Had it not been for the presence of Eryn Rose, Renbourne would surely have wept. The eagerness in his wife's sea-green eyes and the tremor in her hands that was now more pronounced than ever, fixed him where he sat. It was as if he were watching her through the glass of a display case in a museum. But he could see that his daughter was fully wowed by what she had heard, as if it had confirmed something she already knew.

"When will I be an angel, mummy? When? When?"

"Oh darling, one day you will be! Just like your mummy and your daddy. We will start something that will spread across the world. There will be angels everywhere and it will go on forever."

"How are we to do that Suzie?" managed Renbourne at last, reaching forward and taking his wife's trembling hand in an attempt to stay it; but her tremor merely spread through him until he too shook a little.

"Eryn Rose, darling – run and get Mummy some paper and a pencil. Quick now."

Eryn Rose did as she was told and returned excitedly some moments later with her drawing pad and a blue pencil. Suzanne closed her eyes and drew slowly for no more than thirty seconds. Looking at what she had produced she smiled and presented it triumphantly to her husband and her daughter.

"Wings," stated Renbourne, glibly.

"Not just wings, Daddy. They're angel wings!"

"That's right sweetheart. That's what me and daddy are going to get. You will get yours when you're older."

"Yay!" Eryn hugged her mum as her dad looked on at them both with a mixture of awe and tiredness.

Within a week both Suzanne and Renbourne had the angel wings tattooed on their legs to the exact design Suzanne had drawn that night – one on the back of each calf. It was Renbourne who came up with the name Eastern Region Angel Collective. His ailing wife infused him with her spirit and they would talk long into the nights, when she was able, about how throughout the country there would one day be pockets of angels, Collectives, who would bring hope to the downtrodden, turn around the lives of the beaten and in so doing change the world.

Pearly Spencer, a local homeless man, had been the first project for the Eastern Region Angel Collective. It was during their work with him and later with his input that they developed the techniques that would be used thereafter – the four sessions, the written messages, the tasks and the instillation of a belief that everybody is wonderful. There had been no refinement necessary over the years. From that first moment, Suzanne knew what she was doing. For she was working from a vision – surely the finest blueprint there is.

Just two weeks after Pearly had moved back to live with his wife in Cambridge, Suzanne passed away. Of all the people at the funeral, it was Renbourne and Eryn Rose who were the calmest. Such had been the impact Suzanne's courage had made on the hospital staff that there were nurses and doctors in attendance who cried as if she had been one of their own. But they hadn't known she was an angel who saw visions. Neither were they aware of the Eastern Region Angel Collective, an organisation that would take thirteen years before increasing its numbers once more back to two.

Never was anyone more suited to the role of an angel than Eryn Rose. And never did a son miss his mother more than Brando. She had died a week before his third birthday. What irked him more than anything else was the feeling he had been born too late. Eryn Rose would often recount 'The Angel Plan', as she used to call it, and the fact that she was a part of it, how she had fetched the paper and watched her mother draw the wings and how she was told that she would be an angel one day too; thinking all along that she was helping her younger brother to understand more about their mother. But all it

147

did was remind Brando that he had missed out – and that nobody had said that he would one day be an angel. To his eternal regret he had slept all the way through the whole thing, only really waking up twenty-seven years later having stepped off the plane at Stansted Airport, his Irish love dream in tatters.

It was then that he had gone to see his father and asked to be a part of the Eastern Region Angel Collective. Reluctantly, Renbourne had assented to his request, pending a trial period. Brando had not followed through with anything he had started in his whole life, be it homework, after-school clubs, courses, jobs or relationships. He had just drifted through without commitment or direction, hence Renbourne's reticence to add another member to the group even though it be his own son. But, in late January 2011, he had given Brando a chance to earn his angel wings.

Almost immediately Brando had found himself to be of some use in generating business by a chance encounter whilst he was in town. He had been wandering around looking for someone that may be in need of an angel when he heard a screech that all but set him running.

"Brando!! Hiii!!"

Such was the volume of the salutation, several people who weren't named Brando turned in the direction from whence the voice had come. Brando did all he could to ignore it and continued to walk on. When he heard the tottering click-clack of high-heels on stone however, he knew he had no choice but to come to a halt. A fog of perfume smothered him before he had even turned round. Gassed by Boots the Chemist. Such is the modern way. And there she was, Evangeline, giggling receptionist at Essex Probation, ex-girlfriend of Brando Anderson and a history of overdosing whenever a relationship failed – which was frighteningly often.

"Evangeline," Brando murmured, trying to breathe the crisp March air through the fragrant fumes of his assailant.

"Brando! Brando! Come on! You must have coffee with me! Coffee and cake! Or hot chocolate! Hot chocolate and cake! Come on!"

She grabbed his hand and he stumbled after her to a café around the corner just at the edge of one of the two indoor shopping centres. He thought for a moment that he could see make-up dripping off her face as a consequence of her frenetic movement. It was like being a carriage hitched to a novelty-cake train. If children had clambered up her legs and taken chunks out of her he would not have been at all surprised. There was nobody like Evangeline. Nobody in real life anyway.

In spite of the weather, Evangeline insisted on one of the round aluminium tables outside the front of the café. The aluminium chairs were more suited to children than to grown adults and the four legs each seemed to be entirely of different lengths. The discomfort Brando felt being in the present company was only exacerbated by the instability of the chairs. A young man in black came out to take the order and was clearly pleased to return to the warmth of the café, his hind quarters having been thoroughly assessed by Evangeline and deemed 'adequate'.

When their drinks arrived, the first thing Evangeline did was to pluck a pink marshmallow from the frothy cream head of her hot chocolate and rest it briefly upon her tongue before reeling it in. Brando just tried to conceal as much of himself as possible behind the enormous white mug of black coffee he held in both his hands.

"So how have you been, Evangeline?" he asked, tentatively.

"Oh fine," she replied. "I've got a new boyfriend now. I hope you don't mind. It's been what, six months, since us? I tried to wait longer, I really did but well I keep getting all these offers from all these men and I can't cry over you forever, not that I really cried. I was upset as you know and I'm sorry about all those text messages but they did help me get over you quicker. That's what the girls said. It was like a way of moving on. That's what they said as well. I didn't mean those things I called you in the texts. It was just, what did Sandy call it? Bereavement, that's it. And now I'm all better and anyway how are you?"

And she hadn't even swallowed the marshmallow. She had lodged it in her left cheek all the while she'd been talking. Only now did she ease it out slowly with her tongue before opening her mouth briefly and swallowing it, licking her lips like a porn star.

"I'm alright," replied Brando. There was something about her that still attracted him. He just couldn't put his finger on it. Perhaps it was the way she licked her lips like a porn star. She didn't give him the chance to consider the point further.

"So what are you doing with yourself? Are you with someone? Come on – you must be!"

Brando shook his head thinking of Irish rain and silence and cold windows.

"Well if you won't tell, you won't tell! Are you still at college doing the business thing?"

"No. I've got a job now."

"Ooh! What is it? Are you getting lots of money?"

A couple who had been sitting at an adjacent table, the only other people who had decided to brave the chill, discreetly moved inside, having been thoroughly evangelined.

"To be honest, I can't really talk about it. I shouldn't even have mentioned it."

Brando took a sip of his coffee. Evangeline's eyes widened. A perfectly round black hole appeared between her lips. Her hot chocolate was going cool but her libido certainly wasn't.

"I won't tell anyone," she whispered, leaning forward. "I promise."

Looking over his shoulder and then back at Evangeline's smitten, adoring face, Brando addressed her.

"There might be something you could do for me." His voice was low and pitched perfectly at a murmur. Evangeline cocked her head like a golden retriever who had just thought it had heard, far away, the word *walkies*. "You still work at Probation, right?"

Evangeline nodded.

"Well my 'organisation' works in certain 'areas' that cross your territory. Having someone on the inside could be very useful. To both our masters."

If Evangeline could have got away with throwing herself topless over the table at that point she would have done. Rapt does not begin to describe it.

"If ever you have any information for me, call me on this number." He wrote his new mobile number on the napkin and slid it across the table to her. She quickly put it in her bright green handbag and snapped it shut immediately.

"What sort of information?" she whispered again.

"Specifically what we're looking for is people that could be dangerous to the public, people like the ones who come into your offices but who, when they've done their time with you, give you the feeling that they're still not right. You know what I mean, you're a clever girl. That's what we need, people who on the surface seem reasonable but you know deep down that they are capable of anything. Just give me whatever you can, no matter how big or how small."

It was that final word that led Evangeline to snap open her bag and take out her eyebrow pencil. She grabbed her napkin and wrote upon it. The whole action complete within just a few seconds.

Brando lifted the napkin and read the words – *Rod Langford. Roddy.* He pushed back his chair, put the napkin in his pocket and walked around to Evangeline to whisper into her ear. "Text me where he lives, where he drinks, a description – that's important – and anything else you can find out. But keep it between us."

And Evangeline, well, I should imagine she still hasn't stopped quivering from that day to this. But true to her word she was able to give Brando the name of the street where Rod lived and, knowing the area, she hazarded a guess that he would drink in The Setting Sun. This was sadly followed up by several text messages imploring him to have his way with her to which he never replied. This in turn was followed by a period of 'bereavement' texts, which was only 'natural and healthy' of course given the circumstances.

19. The Deep Soul Bliss Of The Truly Cool

"So they are the rules," stated the grizzled looking man in full army regalia complete with two medals and a red bandana. "Any questions soldiers?"

The ragtaggle battalion of twenty men that stood in line before him remained silent. Some shook their heads, others just looked down. Ray and Danny were doing their absolute best to supress a giggle that had started when the commanding Sergeant by whom they had just been addressed had managed to proclaim the immortal lines:

"We're all adults here. All men of the world. And you need to know one thing and I want you to understand it *very* clearly. Anybody, and I mean *anybody*, who fires at any one of my marshals will feel my red balls in their face so fast they will be screaming in agony before they know what's happened."

The marshals explained the equipment to the two teams and they all loaded up with red and yellow paintballs, paint-bombs and guns. Visors in place, the games began – five in all. If it wasn't for the colours of the respective team armbands it would have been impossible to tell who was on which side. Except for Rod of course. His height marked him out for special ridicule and attention from the opposition. Yet during the first four games he hadn't been hit once. Coming to the decider, many of the men were tired, muddy, sweaty and thirsting for beer. The score was tied at two games apiece. The winning team stood to win a crate of lager and a half-price voucher for a future excursion. Ah, the spoils of war.

The final game was called "Bridge Over Troubled Waters". In fact each of the games had been named by the battle-hardened Sergeant after various Simon and Garfunkel songs. The Moon & Sixpence team had been victors in "Homeward Bound" and "Slip Slidin' Away" but had been soundly beaten in "Somewhere They Can't Find Me" and "Flowers Never Bend With The Rainfall."

The idea of the last game, like those that preceded it, was to capture the flag and return it to your base. The tricky part about 'Bridge Over Troubled Waters' was the fact that the flag fluttered from the middle of a narrow wooden bridge which spanned a dark, dank pool. To call it 'troubled' was being, in truth, a little kind – 'disgusting' would have been a more apt adjective, but nowhere near as poetic perhaps.

Each end of the pool was home to one or other of the team bases with a bedraggled copse of trees on either side of the pool giving scant protection. There was a time limit of thirty minutes to the final game – thirty minutes left of what had at first seemed like a fine idea. But like so many fine ideas, this too had the potential to be remembered for nothing more than the intensity of the misery that only a loving spouse back at a campsite can bestow. But there was still time to turn it all around. There's always time to turn it around.

The Sergeant had called on the men to show one last dash of heroism, though privately he had already decided that not one of them was worthy of the uniform. The two teams and their marshals trudged off to their bases and discussed tactics.

The marshal that had been allocated to the Moon & Sixpence team, Karl, did his best to instruct his troops as they sat before him in a semi-circle. He didn't have the battle weary bravura of the Sergeant, yet there was clearly a keen rivalry between him and the other marshal that evidently led to him feeling the need to galvanise his men with a final inspirational call to arms.

"We need to win this one lads to carry the day. Do it for me and for yourselves. That bastard up the other end knocks his girlfriend about. Everyone knows it except for her. I should know. I've been putting her away the last three months. So let's not just do this to win a spawny game of paintball and a crate of warm beer – let's do it for that woman. Let's do it for all women. And let's do it for justice!"

Now it wasn't quite Henry V but, in its own way, it suited the occasion. Having set the tone for battle, Karl squatted down to be at the same level as his soldiers.

"Right. Tactics. This game usually ends in a stalemate. Going for the flag on the bridge leaves you totally exposed. Picking them off behind their barricade is no good – would take too long. We've only got half an hour remember. The only chance is for a diversionary tactic. I need three of you to run up one side to draw their fire whilst two more of you peg it down the other side and hope that one of you gets to the flag. We then need two relay runners to back you up so if you get shot you throw the flag in their direction, they pick it up and get back here. The two of you that are left, you just guard the base and lay down suppressing fire when necessary."

"Sounds like a good plan," said Paul, nodding.

"It's the best there is," replied Karl, getting to his feet.

"Has it ever worked before?" asked Ray.

"Nope. But it's the only one we have. This is the day it all comes together. I can feel it in my blood." Karl had grown into the role of marshal over the previous few weeks and secretly wished, not for the first time, that he had a gun in his hand. "Remember that poor woman boys and let's bring that flag back home for her!"

Danny and Rod agreed to guard the base whilst Ray and Alex joined Little Frank as the sacrificial raiders down the right flank. Paul and Tim decided to be the ones that would go for the flag with Geoff and Big Frank providing the relay back-up.

The teams took up their positions just as the Sergeant blew three blasts of his regimental horn to signal the commencement of battle.

Almost immediately the air around the Moon & Sixpence base was filled with the cracking, clattering and splattering of paintballs against the rickety wooden barricade. Yellow paint spattered the trees and hearts began to beat that bit faster. It seemed the opposition's tactics were to pin them down from the start with the aim of lowering both morale and courage. But they hadn't bargained with Little Frank. Before Ray and Alex knew what was happening the lad had made a dart for it through the trees! They scrambled to their feet and took off

155

after him, stumbling, crouching, lying low and then getting up again until the bridge was in reach. There was a thicket of bushes between them and the edge of the pool with a narrow gap through which they could access the bridge. The firing now though was so intense that they daren't even move. All they could hope for was that Paul and Tim had made some progress down the left flank. They lay in the dirt trying to regain their breath, both dying for a fag. Little Frank was beside them, all ginger inferno, looking as if he was about to start spouting red paint from his freckles.

A tense stalemate ensued during which random shots were fired and nobody moved. But first one and then two people from the opposing team stood up behind their barricades, arms aloft, and left the battlefield. Rod had taken them both out. The tide was turning and renewed hope surged through the lads from The Moon & Sixpence. The two early losses though, only seemed to inspire the enemy. A fresh barrage of paintballs slammed into the trees. Little Frank was hit. Alex was hit. And Ray was unable to move from behind the tree that shielded him. Each time he peeked out a yellow blur fizzed by his eye-line. He was all but out of the game. Little Frank stomped off in fury with Alex sauntering behind having lit himself a cigarette, providing the smoke for the ginger fire that burned ahead of him

A cry came from the deep on the left flank and Geoff, having been hit squarely on the visor, stalked unhappily back to base. On being told in no uncertain terms by Karl the marshal that head shots didn't count, he was about to thrust himself gleefully back into the battle when a paintball cracked open painfully on the inside of his left knee. He went down in a brummie heap and punched the sodden ground with his right fist. Unfortunately his anger was repelled by a sharp rock that lingered craftily just below the surface. Lost momentarily for words that would fully express how he felt, he breathed hard and deep and fast doing his best to repel his tears. *Bollocks! Fuck!* Wilfred Owen, he was not.

The flag was still on the bridge and nobody from the other team had yet moved from behind their barricade save the two that had been shot by Rod. Karl looked on pensively as he stood by and surveyed the battlefield, feeling the eyes of the Sergeant upon him even though his superior wasn't even watching, the chip van by the car park serving as a greater allure to the battle-hardened veteran, oblivious to the battled that raged so close by. It was like The Great War all over again. Without the poets, of course.

And just like The Great War, it was a time for working class heroes. The heroism began from an unlikely source. Danny stood up unsteadily and made a run for it to join Ray. He paid no heed to the paintballs that thwacked into him but just kept running. By the time he had reached his mate he was aching and most definitely out of the game having been hit at least nine times. The opposition were yelling, angry that the charging fool hadn't stopped and left the battlefield the moment he'd been hit. Danny shouted out a couple obscenities and, grinning, left the field of battle – downed but with credit – and with just a little more dignity than Little Frank was displaying if the sound of a boot smacking against the surrounding fence was anything to go by.

But something in Danny's effort had pressed a button deep within Rod. The little man threw his gun on the floor and leapt over the wooden barricade before ploughing straight into the dirty, muddy pool. The marshal had never seen anything like it. Danny and Alex watched in awe as Rod swam silently (for though the water wasn't that deep it was deep enough for Rod) towards the bridge. The other team had no idea what the splash had been, so hard had they been concentrating on annihilating Danny and so intense was their fury about having wasted their swiftly diminishing ammunition on him. Silence once again reigned.

Aware that the grand plan was in some jeopardy, Paul and Tim looked at one another. They looked back at Big Frank who lay in the mud several yards behind them – Big Frank the relay man, the soldier who would potentially be the one on whom their whole escapade rested. Then they looked into the dark waters and saw Rod's head just in view, his black hair spread out around him, floating on the surface.

157

And they knew right then who the hero was more likely to be. Without a word to one another they leapt up and ran as fast as they could to the enemy base, firing as they ran and shouting 'Banzai!' like in the old comics. They managed to take out three of the opposition in their suicide run and adjudged it to have been a risk worth taking.

Big Frank still lay in the mud. Then he began to twitch. He thrust his right arm in the air until it was rigid and then started kicking his legs, grimacing and grunting for almost a minute. The Moon & Sixpence marshal removed the bandanna that had been slipping down his forehead all day and flung it to the ground. There are diversions and there are diversions but this Frank bloke had surpassed himself! It wasn't until after the game was done that Little Frank informed everyone that his father suffered from epilepsy and had undoubtedly had a seizure. Now that's taking one in the line of duty.

Ray crept out from behind the bush that had been his barricade for the last fifteen minutes and edged along the side of the lake, crawling on his front. Pretty soon the enemy would realise there were only three of them left – himself, Rod and a clearly bewildered Frank. But not a shot was fired. It seemed that at least three of the enemy had expended their bullets on Danny and those that were left were either too wary or too confused to move. Their confusion was raised to an entirely new level however when they saw the flag plucked from the bridge by an unseen hand. Rod swam underwater, his eyes closed, his chest heaving, holding the flag as he went, his breaststroke taking him closer and closer to home. Opening his eyes as he felt the silt beneath him he saw Ray about ten yards from the base, prostrate on the floor imploring him to throw the flag! He stood up, threw the sodden flag to his friend and turned to face the flurry of bullets that pelted him. He stood up as tall as he had ever stood, his arms outstretched, taking paintball after paintball all heroic and wonderful, stinking of swamp but reeking only of glory.

Meanwhile Ray had placed the flag in the base and cheers like you never heard before went up from the trees and the bushes where the dead had fallen. The sun peered in to take a closer look and lit up the pool of water that had delivered the hero of the day. The trees shrugged their branches and somewhere far off a woman was wondering which of her two marshal lovers would be degrading her that night.

Rod was carried on the shoulders of the men. He was dripping with debris and soaked through. His face was pure delight and his eyes had the glow of wonder about them, the deep soul bliss of the truly cool. Oh he had never felt anything like this, all through the hard times and the yearnings and the burnings and the blamings – through the persecution and prosecution and the brazen disregard that had been handed out to him since the day of his condemnation, the day when he stopped growing and the moment he stopped believing.

The men lowered their hero to the floor and even the other team applauded. The Sergeant, well he had tears in his eyes and a crate of Carlsberg in his arms. He presented it to Rod, took a pace back and saluted. The victorious marshal leaned over and, with a napkin, daintily dabbed the Sergeant's face until not a spot of ketchup remained. He then grinned at the other marshal, curled his thumb and forefinger into an 'O' shape and, shaking it slowly, mouthed the word 'wanker' to his foe.

Some moments just last forever and never pale in the retelling but shine on always because they are truly special. And for those like Rod Langford who could so easily slip between the cracks, just as a succession of disappointments brings despair, so it only takes one or two magic times to turn a potential murderer into a lover of this strange life. But these things don't work in isolation. The world turns regardless. Just as one person may find the will to cling on and indeed grow, another may seek the dark swampy depths with all the relief of a homecoming.

159

20. You Have Left The Building

It had been something of a few weeks for Rod Langford. He had been ministered to by an angel and had gained the friendship of the finest friends a man could have. The ruminations that had tortured him in prison and that had grown to overwhelm him on the outside had been quelled purely by companionship and affection. For the first time since he was a small child he had known what it was to be connected to this life, this society and this enduring, evolving marvel that is humanity. But what of his wife, Liz, the woman who had vowed in that registry office just a few years ago to give him those very same things, provide him with all that he had so recently just discovered?

Well she had made her own discovery. She was back at home sitting on her bed reading the three messages that Eryn Rose had sent Rod, messages that he clearly felt had been hidden from her view, having put them in amongst some old bank statements and thrust far enough under the bed as to be out of reach. But you see with change can come suspicion and with suspicion a nagging jealousy that can instil a level of tenacity that is very hard to quell. It is one hell of an itch that until you have looked through every drawer and every pocket, searched thoroughly in every cupboard and under the bed, will just not abate.

Other than his two months in Prison, Rod had never been away from Liz for more than a day since they'd been together. He had never seemed so content or been so frequently absent. He had even enquired after Jasmine's health. All Liz could smell was guilt – the guilt of a man.

Liz read the messages four times in all, placing each sheet of paper gently on the quilt once she'd read it, then turning the pile over and starting again. Finally she folded the papers neatly and inserted them back in amongst the bank statements. Her face had been entirely expressionless whilst reading, indeed, emotion rarely entered those eyes or toyed with that mouth. It had more or less given up making an impact on her outward countenance. That didn't mean that she was devoid of all feeling. Far from it. It's just that she had learned to compartmentalise her emotions - this box for fear, this one for desire, this for anger and so on. But for now those thoughts would have to wait within the well of her mind, for a little while at least. Time was ticking. It was half past seven on Sunday evening. And she had a date.

As Rod was getting himself cleaned up at The Moon & Sixpence, so Liz stepped naked from the bedroom and into the bathroom where a red hot shower awaited. She felt the water slap hard onto every part of her body. Steam rose like clouds and her skin glowed scarlet. If you had been present and looked through the clear plastic glass of the shower door you may well have thought you were looking at the burning eye of a smouldering dragon.

Liz dried herself roughly, dressed in a short black skirt and a white blouse, let her hair hang loose and gazed at herself in the bedroom mirror. Brando knocked at the door. Liz continued to look at herself just a moment longer before letting the would-be angel into her abode.

That afternoon Renbourne, Brando and Eryn Rose had discussed where they were in the case so far.

"So Eryn," began Renbourne, "you were saying Rod didn't show for the final session?"

"It seems he's gone away with some of the people from the pub. That could be a good thing."

"That he didn't show?"

"That he has people to go away with. He didn't really have any friends before. Now he has some. I think that's progress. And he did complete the tasks I set him, remember? And the final session can be re-arranged. I don't think he's as dangerous as we first thought. I haven't had any problems with him, any feeling that he is anything other than a little lonely and a little self-conscious. Having friends and that bit more confidence now, well, it's definitely what he's needed. I still do want to see him for that final session though, just to finish things off, to say goodbye. I've grown quite fond of him to be honest!"

"Brando?" said Renbourne, trying so hard to modulate his voice so as not to infer admonishment. Had he sung a lullaby, however, his son would have still seen it as the harshest of condemnations.

"I've met Liz Langford twice and I plan to meet her again this evening. She's nothing, nothing at all. It was Eryn Rose that said she was worried about her which is the only reason I've been involved at all. I just gave you the referral. You're the one that said it seemed appropriate. Don't have a go at me just because this little bloke didn't need anything other than a few mates to drink with. If you want to point the finger at anyone, point it at your can-do-nothing-wrong daughter."

Renbourne sighed and rubbed his forehead with his left hand, a habit he had acquired over the years to somehow try and assuage his frustration and to signal to his wife, wherever she may be, that despite everything he was still doing his best.

"Brando," said Eryn Rose, aware that her father could not possibly respond. "This is not about winning and losing. It's not about us. It's about helping people and it's about mum."

"Yeah, well I need to get going," replied Brando. And he left the kitchen and went upstairs. Eryn Rose and Renbourne both anticipated the slamming of some door or other but that anticipation did nothing to lessen the disappointment they both felt when a few moments later the front door banged shut and Brando was gone.

"Dad," began Eryn Rose.

Renbourne, head still bowed, raised a hand. "I know," he said. "I know. It's ok, Eryn Rose. It will all be ok."

"But..."

"Not now darling. I'm so tired. Anyway, shouldn't you be off to work?"

Eryn Rose sighed, kissed her still seated father on the forehead and went upstairs to change into the uniform she wore for eighteen hours per week in her role of domestic at Woody Grove Nursing Home in Maldon. She had been working there for thirteen years - and it was at Woody Grove that she most felt like an angel. In truth, these outside cases, such as Rod, were very rare. It was to the people who lived in the home who were ever the main focus of her angelic ministrations.

The residents at Woody Grove experienced, to various degrees, symptoms of dementia. This could range from disorientation to memory loss and, at times, impulsive acts of aggression. Some residents exhibited one or two of these symptoms though it is fair to say that by the time they had been residents for a few months many exhibited all three. This was more to do with the insidious progression of the condition than the care they received at the home. Woody Grove in fact had an excellent reputation, particularly with regard to the management of aggressive outbursts. It was staffed mainly by unqualified staff although there was always at least one nurse on duty in order to give out the medication.

Eryn Rose had seen many people come and go during her time at Woody Grove – both those who worked there and those who lived there. As was true of much of her life, she loved every minute of it, whether she was washing down the skirting boards, polishing the bedside cabinets or picking up food from the floor.

Red is not what it once was, a colour, a warning – it's now a pain, an emotion that grabs me then hurls me across this room where they put me; whoever they are. I'm not hungry. It's light but no I'm not hungry. And I don't need you to feed me. I don't want you to feed me. Ah but there's Elvis again in my ears rocking and grooving and making me dance and I can't help but smile but my dancing now is just so slow. Someone I don't know or maybe just don't remember gets up to hold my hands. Does she want to dance with me, pull me over, push me down? I can't tell these days for there is a mist about me always. Where there once were sharp edges, there is now just all this softness, this muffled and damp softness that hinders me in a way I can't comprehend. I know what I want to say but all you hear is a gargle. I know what I want to do but then it just goes, leaves me like Elvis did – without warning and without replacement. These days and nights are just light and dark to me and I sleep so often yet it's so hard to find rest without you beside me my darling. Tears are all I have for you now. There is no going back from this. I want to hold you but somehow you either slip through my fingers or you back away. And then I find myself sleeping again. These aren't days – it is just one extended period of time that I am made to endure. Yet there are times when Elvis sings and I smile and there are times when I am hungry and I so love my food. But I don't want to be fed. I don't need to be fed. Let me get my dinner all over my face and down my jumper and maybe sometime, by luck and by joy, it might even go where it is intended to go. Rather that than them hold a quivering plastic spoon to my mouth. Rather that than anything. There is an angel here with wings. She soothes me and dries my tears and she would let me feed myself I know it. She reminds me of you. Wherever you are. Wherever you be. Oh my God, I love you. But you have left the building.

Liz and Brando sat at a back corner table in The Setting Sun. Apart from Derek in his usual place at the bar and Sean of course, the pub was empty. The V Festival was reaching a climax in Highlands Park and the music could be heard from the beer garden. Some weary folk had been scattered amongst the tables early in the morning partaking of 'The Best V Breakfast in Chelmsford' The banner at the front of the pub and the all year round Christmas lights that hung beneath it were as deceitful as one another in terms of their promise of wonder. The sausages were microwaved along with the bacon, the egg was scrambled with nothing but anger and the fried bread was just the off-cuts of a stale loaf lathered with twice-used oil. But a hungry raver is a hungry raver and Sean always made a smart profit on V weekend despite the lack of alcohol consumed on the premises. With Ray, Danny and Alex being absent however, the landlord was perhaps even more grim than usual.

"Thank you for seeing me, Liz."

Liz made no reply but just stared a little more intently at Brando from above the glass that was then fully covering her mouth. She swallowed the coke loudly and placed the glass back down before her. Her lips moved towards one another perhaps more slowly than was natural and she eventually blinked at their closing as if the two acts were linked by a single mechanism.

"Rod is seeing someone else," she said.

"How do you mean?" was Brando's immediate reply.

"I found some letters."

"What kind of letters?"

"Love letters."

When Liz spoke the word 'love' there was something about the change in her tone, the effort it took, that seemed to Brando as if she were clearing her throat of some irritation.

"Love letters?"

Liz nodded. "They might as well be."

"To Rod or from Rod?"

"To him."

"Does he know you know about them?"

Liz shook her head.

"Are you going to tell him?"

Again she shook her head. "Can I have another coke?"

Relieved at the prospect of a break in the conversation, Brando went to the bar. They had been talking for less than a minute it had already begun to drain him in some way. He had felt nailed to the chair not just by her stare but by the way she delivered her sentences.

Leaving the table Brando felt as if he had pushed through a thick web and back out again into the open world that everybody else inhabited. But he knew, if ever he was going to prove his father wrong and finally become the angel he knew he could be, that he would have to go back to Liz and see this thing out. Fortified, he returned with a coke for her and another cider for himself.

"So who are the letters from?" asked Brando, tentatively. "Anyone you know?"

"It doesn't matter," replied Liz in the same atonal voice. "I put them back anyway. It's enough that I know."

"What are you going to do?"

Tears came to Liz's eyes and she literally shook. Brando leaned forward and took the glass of coke from her hand so she didn't continue to spill it. Sounds long hidden burst through her lips like bubbles escaping a fizzed up can. Eventually she slowed down, came to a halt and resumed as much as she could her former dour demeanour. Derek and Sean had watched the whole thing but turned away the moment Liz looked in their direction – a crack of a lipstick smile upon her face.

Liz leaned towards Brando and he could not help but lean back a little.

"I'm sorry," she whispered. "It must be the coke."

"Nothing to apologise about," replied Brando. It was then that he put out a hand. It was an entirely unconscious act. To the onlooker, of whom there were two, it seemed perhaps that Liz had reached out to Brando with her own hands simultaneously. However it happened, before he knew what to do, Liz had his hands trapped between hers.

"Oh I'm not worried," said Liz. "It's not me that should be worried. I've got nothing to worry about. Not me."

Brando, perhaps through instinct, told Liz that he needed to go to the toilet, withdrew his hand, stood up and walked to the bathroom on the left just before the exit to the beer garden. Sean took the opportunity to collect the empty glasses from their table.

"Done?" he murmured, not looking at Liz.

"I want you to do something for me," she replied.

Sean looked straight at her, intoxicated by her perfume, stunned by her gaze, invigorated by her words and warmed by her coldness.

Having delayed his return as long as he could, Brando made his way back to the table to find Liz and Sean conversing in subdued tones. He hung back just out of view but could hear nothing. Derek caught his eye but Brando could read nothing from the regular's expression. Perhaps there had been no communication in the look, just the countenance of a man who had spent most of his entire life looking at the interior of various pubs whilst thinking about everything but what he saw.

At last, Sean picked up the two empty glasses and resumed his place behind the bar. Brando resumed his seat. Derek drank up, said his farewells to Sean and left. There are some times when experience tells you it's time to go home.

"Well," said Liz, her face full of colour, her lips bright red and her eyes absolutely gleaming with gleam. "What now?" She put out a hand and brushed her palm slowly against Brando's left cheek. He didn't resist and he didn't move.

All he could say was: "It's up to you."

And how right he was.

21. Blisters And Vision

Sean Parsons had suffered many losses in his life. You may think therefore that the theft of an old washing machine minus its door and filled with a small quantity of drugs may have been a loss with which he could have coped, particularly with it having occurred at the same time that his mother had passed away – perspective and such like. But idioms are idioms and proverbs are proverbs for a reason, surviving centuries of human endeavour, misfortune and confusion to remain as true in this modern world of computers, commerce and capitalism as ever they were in former times. The apposite proverb with regard to the theft of the washing machine would undoubtedly be: *the straw that broke the camel's back.*

There had ever been in Sean's mind a bar in Spain with his name on it. He had pictured it for the entire twenty years he had been in the pub trade. 'Parsons' it would be called, and it would be in a sedate village far away from the towns and the cities. It would attract gentlemen and businessmen, people of class. There would be no fights and no fruit machines and no police raids. It would be a place that people would only know about by word of mouth, a secret, wonderful establishment for the English ex-patriots and the more discerning European traveller. In time he would develop a restaurant business, perhaps next door or upstairs, with the finest, freshest seafood being its speciality. And before long perhaps he would supervise the construction of a small Villa where he would stay with invited guests, special guests, who would partake of the food in his restaurant and the wine at his bar before spending the night beneath the Spanish stars and the morning in the Spanish seas. Thus he would retire one day, perhaps, with a young bride in possession of a lovely figure but perhaps also a facial blemish, such as a birthmark or a burn, who could speak English only sparingly. They would never argue and they would live the remainder of their days in the knowledge that each had done as well in this life as ever was possible.

Yet Sean found himself, after hours in The Setting Sun, pondering the words of a woman just above midget-height, a woman who had transfixed him completely. For the man who is fully aware that his dreams will never come true, the opportunity to participate in the infliction of misery upon another can be a fine consolation indeed. It is a sad truism that there are more people on this earth inclined far more to unpleasantness than to forgiveness. Sean Parsons was clearly such a man - and he most certainly had an eye for those who shared his bitter sensibilities.

Sean's first marriage had ended in tatters on finding out his betrothed had been seeing somebody else for at least a year before they actually got married. His second marriage had ended in Stanford-Le-Hope – as marriages are prone to do. So his faith in the female kind had diminished from an admittedly low starting point to somewhere well below zero. But this Liz Langford, she wasn't like the rest. There was something about her that intrigued Sean, set him to thinking that perhaps his days in Spain may be better off with her than with the facially disfigured, diction disabled woman of his dystopian dreams.

"It's your mother, Mr Parsons," the nurse had said. "We're moving her to the Hospice this afternoon."

Sean had nodded.

"Mr Parsons?"

"Yes. Sorry. I'll be up by the evening. What's the Hospice address?"

The nurse had reeled off the address as if it were her own.

"So she's going to die then?" Sean had asked.

The nurse had nodded, which had been of no use to the man on the other end of the phone. Yet her silence was answer enough.

Sean had hung up.

And out the back of The Setting Sun a washing machine containing a reasonable amount of assorted drugs had been loaded into the back of a van by an opportunist driver who would never know the chain of events he had set in motion.

"Do you have to be back any particular time?" asked Liz as she brought a bottle of wine from the small kitchen to the lounge and topped up Brando's already full glass.

"No," replied Brando. "I just need to know you're okay and then my job is done."

Liz sat down beside him on the sofa.

"And just what exactly is your 'job'?" she asked, staring at the side of his face, filling him with her entire being. Had he turned to face her at that moment he surely would have exploded in all sorts of ways – none of them good.

"Like I said. My people have been worried about Rod and my role is just to make sure you're okay. They're not worried about him anymore now though. But they obviously don't know about what you told me earlier. Him seeing someone else and stuff."

"And where does that leave *us*?" asked Liz, placing a hand on Brando's right thigh.

Brando had never been stabbed but knew that instant what it felt like, cold and numb and hard and scarred and bound to the ground and deaf to the sound of all other life within a hundred miles. Had he not been sitting he would have fallen.

All he could say was: "Us?"

He made the fatal mistake of turning to face her. From that very moment his clock was ticking. It was as if she had transformed. Her eyes had got wider in the middle and narrower at the edges and her mouth was just a big red mass of incessant suction. Her hands clamped the back of his head in a robotic clamp and it seemed like hours before he was allowed to come up for air.

"Hang on, hang on, hang on," he said finally, using up more or less all the oxygen he had just acquired, unaware as to how he had

170

possibly been able to extricate his lips from hers. Liz gazed at him as if she'd just performed some incredible feat of magic and was daring him to deny that what he had experienced was real. "I need to go now. My work here is done," he said.

"Your work here is done?" replied Liz, leaning back, daring him.

Brando stood, picked his jacket up from the floor and thrust his arms through it as if he were punching the air.

"Your work here is done?" Liz repeated, staying seated.

"Rod's alright. You're alright – well except for the affair thing. I know you said about those letters and that, but you know, Rod was our case and it's over. He's been sorted. That's our job. That's my job. We sort. It's done. Look. I have to go. It would be unprofessional of me to stay."

"Unprofessional?"

As Liz made to rise so Brando made for the door. He got there first. As Liz gained her full, yes, full height, the closing of the front door resounded about the small flat. It was only one of his business cards resting where he had sat, giving his full address and phone number that enabled Liz to come back into the light from the dark that had ever been so becoming.

The computer by the door hummed, beckoning Liz towards it. She had never really used it before. It had always been Rod's domain. But things change and that is life. When she stood before it and moved the mouse the screen flashed into being. Of the few icons before her it was the one entitled 'wideawake' that drew Liz to it. She double-clicked the icon and slowly read the words that appeared before her. Then she began to type. And, in doing so, many a fate was sealed.

The Eastern Region Angel Collective. The E.R.A.C. - CARE backwards. An anagram of RACE – meaning speed and progress and inclusion. Eryn Rose had grown up with the belief that her mother and father had created an organisation that spread nationwide, a network of angels who strove to repair the lives of the unfortunate and to do the good work that others failed, or were not allowed, to do. There was the Western Angel Contingent, the North Western Angels and the North Eastern Angel Collective and, in the centre, the Midlands Angel Alliance. Not a tenuous acronym among them worthy of the Eastern Region Angel Collective. Oh to grow up knowing your mother was a saint and your father was the very foundation of all that secretly kept this nation going. That is a privileged upbringing indeed.

"Daddy, Daddy, can you tell me some more about the angels? Who have they saved today?"

"You have school tomorrow Eryn Rose. It really is time for bed. We can have more about the angels tomorrow night."

"Oh Daddy, just one more. I promise I'll go to sleep after. I promise!"

"Just one then. Just one…"

It could have been the tale of the man who had lost his job and had been instructed by an angel to pursue his dreams of wood-carving and then managed to construct such a wonderful piece of art that it was lauded around the world as the finest sculpture made from wood that had been seen for many a year. But then the angel had re-appeared and spoke to the man of things such as integrity and destiny and fortitude and beauty and the man had reclaimed his sculpture reforming it into a heart that only he and the angel understood. For the heart was in the shape of a bird that nobody sees.

Or it could have been the story of the family who had no money for food but who decided to grow their own sustenance from seeds and would open up their garden every year to the needy and the hungry, the destitute and the poor who would avail themselves of the goods that were on offer. And anything that was left over was distributed around the world by the bird that nobody sees.

Maybe even it was the recounting of the history of hope. How the bird that nobody sees carried it from land to land over sea and ocean, gleaming with glory and replete with completeness – shimmering shiny in the doom of the gloom and bursting into our lives with a consciousness that is only worthy of the honest and the plain.

The bird that nobody sees gives flight when your feet are but blisters and vision when you can see no more. And it gets you through your childhood when you've lost your mum. That's the bird that nobody sees.

There was not a teacher at Boswell's School that could convince Eryn Rose that her studies had any value. What use is chemistry when you know you are going to be an angel? What good is there in learning mathematics when the role in life for which you are destined is not made up of numbers but of love?

Many a time did Renbourne attend a parents evening and come away questioning himself. As a single male parent the odds and the trust were already stacked heavily against him. But what the authorities hadn't reckoned with was the love he still had for Suzanne and the determination he had that their daughter would grow to be an angel.

As it was, Eryn Rose attained seven GCSEs and the entry requirement to Palmer's College in Grays – the reward for which was three hours at a tattoo parlour beneath a bridge on Southend Sea Front where she received, on the back of each calf, her angel's wings. Though they were but ink they elevated her to the heavens. And she had never once been inclined to come back down.

My name is Eryn Rose and Eryn Rose I am. I've been the age I am now since the day I was born, which was just yesterday or tomorrow - I can't remember which. My hair is fair and my eyes are blue green oceans or brown workingmen's soil just whenever they need to be. I dance when I can and I walk with a sway that comes from the breeze and the seas and the albatross wings that sing a song you all can hear better than me.

Each day is fresh to me and the air is not just there it is a bonus, a wonder, a scrummy yum of perfect life that I take in with delight and breathe out with a delicious sigh. My nerves zing and zang and the softness of my skin is just my heart really. I wear nothing on my feet (except for my toes of course!) as I like to be as close to the earth as I can even if there's a carpet or concrete or the scrimble scramble crumble of debris and refuse beneath my footsies and my tootsies.

I am an angel within the Eastern Region Angel Collective. My father is an angel too and so was my mother. They are the ones who formed this network, this group of angels that covers the whole of England. There are literally hundreds of us doing the work that keeps people going. But it's not work! What am I saying?! How can what I do be called work? What I do is just breathing with words. There is no effort in that. I learned that from when I was small. Kindness is as natural as lifting your hand to the sun to feel its warmth, as natural as closing your eyes so as to better take in the fragrance of the sweetest scent. That's not work, it's just life.

My dad co-ordinates all the angel activity – he draws up charts and plans and diagrams. He keeps records and statistics in all sorts of colours in a filing cabinet in his room. From as far back as I can remember I can see him sitting at the table in the kitchen writing and thinking and staring into his own space. I would tug at his arm and he would look down at me when I was small or up at me if it is in recent times. I used to think he had been crying but I know now that it's just the overwhelming feeling we angels get when we reflect upon what we do. And that's why we don't like to talk about it, even with each other. The next step is pride and with pride comes superiority and thereafter it's just a few steps to arrogance. And before you know it you have a religion. That's what dad used to say: Don't talk about it. Don't tell anyone. This isn't a religion.

Part of being an angel is knowing that what you do is as normal as saying good morning to a stranger or giving what money you have to a busker. As normal as that.

Sometimes I just write things like this while I'm sitting in the park and then make a paper airplane out of it and let the words just

go where they will. It's good for people to know that there are angels
around. People have a right to feel safe. Well that's what I think.
Bye!

And sometimes somebody follows you and watches you without you being aware. Then when you go they pick up the piece of paper in the shape of an airplane, unfold it, read it and put it in their pocket. They walk away, again unseen by you because you're on that swing again thinking worthy thoughts, no doubt, whilst so close by you is a person intent only on doing the worst of harm.

22. So Good Morning

The lads returned to Chelmsford early Monday morning. Cars filled with V Festival dregs and worn out weary souls stuttered by on the other side of the road. The warmth of the weekend soon gave way to summertime gloom. The sky was grey and the air was dripping with melancholy. Ray drove back in silence. Danny and Rod dozed in the back seat. Alex had his window down so he could smell the breeze. Nothing was wasted on him, nothing spurned. No beauty went unrecognised – wherever it be.

Alex only lived a few doors down from Ray so they dropped Rod and Danny off first at the junction of Redmayne Drive and Pearce Manor. Their flats were in opposite blocks yet neither had been in the other's home. Danny went left and Rod right as Ray turned the car around and waved to them both. Rod's mind was now reeling not with murderous ambition but with an accumulation of thoughts and experiences that culminated in what might tentatively be called hope. Enlightenment can come in many ways - paintball, cider, mates and the words of a failed and drunken author being just one such combination.

So Ray dropped Alex home, parked outside his own house and finally let himself in. On the table was a note from his wife along with a packet of Dolly Mixtures - his favourites. *"Save me the pink ones!"* read the note. His wife loved him more than anything else either he or she could ever imagine – even more than Dolly Mixtures. And one day, as a token of his love for her, he may even save her the pink ones.

Ray's wife worked as a paediatric nurse in London and often their working schedules would lead Ray and her to seeing each other only for stolen minutes. But that was okay - for love knows not the ticking of a clock but just the beating of hearts. Ray had only in recent years come to understand that. His wife had known it from the moment she had first set eyes on him. She transformed lives you see and Ray's had been a life in need of transformation. What had first struck her about him was the way he would talk of people in his present and his past as if she knew them. He would always use first names and surnames when speaking of the people he knew, almost as if they were famous. But that was the thing with Ray – people were precious, everybody was significant, everybody was famous. There was a depth to everything he did, yet nobody ever knew just how close he came, sometimes daily, to imploding entirely. Except perhaps his wife.

Liz was out with Jasmine when Rod entered the flat. The silence following his clumping stair climb was tangible. It was as if he had just rolled away the stone of a tomb. The air was strange to him, the colours just a shade different from what they ought to be. Yet this was supposed to be his home. Perhaps it was the weekend he had spent in the burst open country or maybe it was just that he was seeing with new eyes now. Everything seemed so very small. And there was not a Dolly Mixture in sight – pink or otherwise.

Rod put his bag down in the bedroom and glanced at the bed he shared with Liz. In just that one quick look he noticed the small card on his pillow. He picked it up and read it.

Brando Anderson – 25 Fletcher Street – 067639237

It was just then, that he heard the key turning in the lock so he sharply replaced the card and tried to put it out of his mind. These were new days, new times, new futures. He breathed deeply to steady the green booming in his chest and walked into the small hallway to greet his wife.

Jasmine yelped a restrained welcome and Liz turned to face Rod.

"You're wearing make-up," was the first thing he said.

"And?"

"You don't wear make-up."

177

"Well now I do," she replied, hanging up the dog lead on the hook by the door. "Hello would have been nice," she added, in a more subdued, less defiant tone.

"Yeah, sorry. Hello. So are you alright?"

"Did you have a good time?"

"It was okay. Good to be back though. So you, you're ok?"

"Why wouldn't I be?"

"No reason. Do you want a coffee or something?" Rod asked, moving into the refuge of the narrow kitchen. "I'm going to have one."

"No, I'm good thanks."

Liz went into the bedroom and almost tripped over Rod's bag. Before going through it though, ostensibly for things that needed washing but more to confirm what she already believed, she put Brando's card in the small drawer in the cabinet on her side of the bed, somewhat amused that the card had obviously been moved. You see if you just put love letters from your lover girlfriend under the bed then you won't know if your wife has seen them – there's no precision in that. A card placed delicately on a pillow however, well, that's how you catchy the monkey. Not that Liz even needed the card – she had memorised the address and the mobile number as if it were her own. And, unlike her clumsy husband, she hadn't even left a fingerprint.

"I'm going to have a bath," called Rod. Liz heard the bathroom door close and the lock slide into place. And there they were, the man and the wife who but a few short weeks ago were what you would have perhaps called 'comfortably married.' Now they were anything but. Both sighed with relief when that bolt slid into its slot even though they hadn't seen each other for three days. That's how love can go sometimes. It's nobody's fault. It's just how love can go.

Rod lay in the warm bath wide-awake, truly wide-awake, at last. Where once he had awoken to the notion that he could take the life of another and be proud of it, he was now awake to the very substance of life itself. It hadn't taken years of psychotherapy or antidepressants or counselling or self-help books or sitting in groups or attending appointments just so his name could be ticked off a list in the name of healthcare. No. It had just come about by his being treated without prejudice and without expectation.

"Fancy a beer? There you go mate."

You see it's each one of us that has it within our power to transform the life of another just by being decent. That's all. You can be from the Eastern Region Angel Collective or you can drink yourself stupid every week in The Setting Sun or The King's Head or wherever you care to drink. It really doesn't matter. It doesn't take any sort of system or qualification or name badge or desk. It just begins with saying good morning to a total stranger.

So good morning.

The bubbles popped against the hair on Rod's legs and he watched, fascinated as they went from something to nothing. He closed his eyes and felt the heat of the water against his skin, how it seemed so heavy yet it moved when he moved and became still just shortly after he became still. It was only when his eyes were closed that he could hear the bubbles pop. He tried to breathe like he'd seen Alex breathe but he ended up just coughing, causing the water to panic and the bubbles to pile upon one another like hordes of translucent children backing away from an unnamed hairy fiend, all clingy and afraid.

Rod opened his eyes and saw that the white tiles around the bath were swathed in a light film of mist and the mirror above the washbasin dripped with cold steam sweat. As the bath-water cooled there was a beautiful moment when Rod realised that both he and the water were of the same temperature and when he closed his eyes once more it was as if he had popped like one of those long-gone bubbles.

Just 'pop' and he was gone.

Liz meanwhile had dialled Brando's number on the house phone eighteen times having entered the prefix that prohibited the caller's number appearing at the other end. And eighteen times she had listened to his voice: "Brando here. Well not here. Obviously. Leave a message and I'll see what I can do…" She had hung up on each occasion without uttering so much as a word.

Just 'pop' and she was gone.

On the other side of town, in the back bedroom of 25 Fletcher Street, Charley Patton was singing to Eryn Rose:

> *Bad luck is at your front door, blues is in your room*
> *Bad luck is at your front door, blues is in your room*
> *I'm knockin' at your back door;*
> *What's gonna become of you?*

Charley Patton was singing in such a growling gravel howl that in the room across the landing Brando Anderson heard it loud and clear. Had Brando been more apprised of the mystical work of the great bluesman then he may well have concluded that there was indeed high water everywhere and that the lyrics were so much more pertinent to *his* well-being than that of his older sister.

Eighteen calls in two minutes. No number left. No message. When you check your phone, which you've switched to silent mode, and are faced with that then it surely gets your mind a-whirring. Evangeline? Not dramatic enough. Liz Langford? She wouldn't know how to get hold of him. Wrong number? Too persistent. So he just lay back on his bed, his thoughts moving slower than he would have liked – more conscious of his propensity for confusion since that forced kiss from Liz – a kiss that had entered him like a miasma. He reached back and scratched his neck almost as if to remind himself that her fingers no longer gripped his nape.

Renbourne too was in his room, downstairs, where he'd converted the small lounge to a study/sleeping area. On the door leading into the study was a laminated sign reading "Eastern Region Angel Collective." Inside, there was just a desk, a fold-up bed, a locked filing cabinet and a low armchair in which he spent most of his day. He always preferred the door closed. Eryn Rose and Brando knew not to knock. When the door was closed he was with Suzanne. It was their time together. Neither Eryn Rose nor Brando had seen anything of what was in the filing cabinet. She had never had the inclination to even sneak a peek. You don't get to be in charge of the biggest network of angels in the country without knowing what you're doing – particularly when you're one of the co-founders.

But there comes a time when even the mighty delta blues of the mighty Charley Patton can feel a little loud. So Renbourne rose unsteadily from his armchair, blinked farewell to the spirit of his wife, opened the study door and climbed the stairs to where his children lay in their rooms.

Eryn Rose's door was always open. She preferred it that way. If she could she would have had the front door of the house open too, so she could forever be connected to the world like a perfect maze from her room to the landing, down the stairs to the hallway and into the streets of Chelmsford and thereon to the crazed meanderings of this wholly incredible universe.

"Eryn Rose, do you mind turning it down a little?"

"Sorry Dad. What time is it?"

"Just gone nine."

"Ok. I need to get some sleep now anyway. Must try and meet up with Rod tomorrow just to finish things off. Night Dad."

And she blew her father the most fairy-winged beautiful butterfly kiss that ever fluttered across a room from daughter to dad. Uncomfortable as he was in the ways of returning affection, Renbourne instead tried to be of use.

"Did you realise," he said, "that Going Up The Country by Canned Heat is probably a complete rip-off of High Water Everywhere by Charley Patton?"

"No I didn't!" Eryn gasped. "Really?"

"Good night darling."

"Night Dad."

181

Renbourne pulled the door gently closed with a click, leaving his gorgeous daughter to rummage through her CD collection in complete awe.

Brando had heard his father approaching and closed his eyes as if asleep. Renbourne steadied himself and looked in briefly at his son before returning back downstairs to his study, Going Up The Country skipping after him from beneath Eryn's door.

Doot doot do-do doo. Doot doot do-do doo…

But Renbourne had no use for skipping or for the country or even heat for that matter, canned or otherwise. He just sat once more in his old armchair, his eyes falling to the desk to his right where an old piece of paper lay sellotaped to the battered wood detailing the basic rules of angels. There were five in total:

1. Do not look directly into the eyes of an angel unless absolutely necessary

2. Do not disclose to anyone the nature of the angel network

3. Do not discuss or draw attention to your tattoos

4. You may introduce yourself to others as an angel if you think it will help

5. Once an angel – always an angel

Suzanne had drawn up the last two rules before she died. Renbourne had subsequently added the first three. The third was to ensure as far as possible that only angels who had earned their wings would have the requisite tattoo on the back of each calf. The second was to make sure that Renbourne maintained control of the various contingents of angels across the country – one of the reasons why only he possessed the key to the filing cabinet in the corner, a cabinet whose four drawers were labelled with the names of each Collective. The first rule was purely for his own self-preservation. For whenever he looked into the eyes of his daughter he saw not her but the wife that he loved beyond, absolutely beyond, compare. Worse still, when he looked into the eyes of his son, he saw just himself – a distraught man seeking salvation.

Unfair on Brando perhaps and undoubtedly a major contributor to the young man's floundering sense of self and of place. Not only had he been too young to be involved in the formation of the Eastern Region Angel Collective, his relationship with his father had been doomed only ever to be tragic.

For the only thing more tragic than not being an angel is to love an angel that is no longer around. Right there and then as he felt a fractious sleep take him, Renbourne knew that he should have added a sixth item to the list. But he was just too weary to do so.

6. Never fall in love with an angel. For it will break your heart.

Whilst Renbourne drifted into sleep, something that he only did when he was thoroughly exhausted, Brando lay wide awake upstairs. The moon was full and big in the late summer sky and the night outside was calm and still. As he stepped quietly downstairs to scribble on a post-it note, he saw that his father's study door was open. More than that, his eyes were drawn to a small silver key, winking in the moonlight, protruding starkly from the lock of the filing cabinet, access to which had ever been forbidden. But the times they were a-changing – and a young man will always desire to know what comes between him and his father.

23. Morphine Wonderland

"Even you would have had a tear in your eye Sean. Honest. It was like something out of Platoon," enthused Danny.

"Yeah, well," replied Sean, "it wasn't real though was it? Not like Platoon."

"Hate to break this to you, mate," said Ray, "but Platoon wasn't real either."

Sean looked over at Ray, knowing through years of miserable experience that a witty riposte was well beyond him. But when wit fails and sarcasm won't even lend a hand, rancour can generally be relied upon to make an appearance with those such as Sean – the resentful, disheartened, maudlin types for whom FRUGALITY would be nothing but a set of capital letters promulgated by a desperate fool in a drunken moment, published as an eBook because no other bugger could make any money out of it.

"Then Platoon must be about as real as your pool team was ever likely to be," retorted possibly the worst landlord in England.

But Ray and Danny weren't even listening. Derek had come in and started telling them how Jimpsy had been arrested the weekend they were away for the assaults on the lads from The Eagle and Hind and was now back in HMP Chelmsford.

It was Tuesday 23rd August and the end of the school holidays was in sight. Ray and Danny would soon be back to the classroom, their Moon & Sixpence army days but an embellished memory to be recalled at times when life just got a little too tough. But The Setting Sun would always be their anchor, their refuge from the pressure and the admonishments and the glares and the stares and the establishment howls.

When you walk into a pub and the first thing you feel is relief then that is a testament to those who have been before you and those that are there still. And if the landlord is a miserable old bastard? Well that's why you have a big old wooden bar to draw the line in the beer-stained sand with a mirror at eye-level behind it to reflect all those about you who understand every deep down feeling you experience although you may not even know their name.

And wouldn't you just know it? Minutes later, in walked Rod, hero of The Battle of Waldringfield Swamp and the most highly decorated marine in Eastern Counties campsite history. Twenty-four cans of lager may not be the Victoria Cross but it's a bloody good start.

Before he could even say hello, Rod was greeted with a raucous chorus of Status Quo's "You're In The Army Now." Even Derek joined in as did a couple that nobody knew, over by the dart board.

"Whoa, whoa, whoa you're in the army now!!"

A round of applause (if five people clapping can indeed be referred to as such) and a round of drinks later, the unknown couple had departed and Sean was just waiting his moment, the words Liz had spoken to him just a few days ago as clear in his consciousness as if her lipstick was still smudged scarlet upon his ear – which indeed it had been up until two hours ago. Whilst Ray and Danny were playing pool Sean leaned over the bar and tapped Rod on the shoulder.

"A word. Out back. Won't take long,"

Rod looked round at his mates as if for advice but Ray had his forehead on the green baize having just potted the white and Danny was in the midst of a frothy bearded chortle.

So Rod had no option but to follow Sean's stain-spattered jogging bottoms out to the beer garden.

Sean lit himself a meagre roll-up and Rod sparked-up a tailor-made. The distinction did not go unnoticed by either of them.

"There's something I've got to say to you, my friend," began Sean – more Godfather than Platoon. "I'm going to say it briefly and I'm only going to say it once." And from Godfather he had sunk to 'Allo 'Allo.

185

Rod looked up at the landlord and tried to counter with his best Taxi Driver.

"You talking to me?" he said.

"Yeah, I'm talking to you. You might have done a bit of time or you might not. I don't rightly care. But when a dame tells me that her man's not treating her right, I got a need to know what sort of man that is."

Humphrey Bogart well and truly turning in his grave, Sean looked down upon his foe.

Undeterred, Rod looked up at Sean fully in the eye. There was neither mate nor angel to be seen. He took one last drag of his cigarette that was still only half burned, spat on the floor and made to go back inside, as close to East of Eden James Dean as James Dean ever got.

"And one more thing," said Sean all Columbo and Hill Street Blues. "Your missus was in here with another bloke at the weekend. Just thought you ought to know."

Rod took his place again at the bar where Ray and Danny were just finishing their pints, their game of pool having ended with the tip of one of the cues having come loose

"You alright mate?" asked Danny.

Rod nodded. "Just Sean being a prick. That's all."

"Three pints here Sean."

"Shake him up a bit" is what Liz had said. *"That's all I need you to do. Just shake him up a bit. It will be worth your while."*

The lipstick on his ear was just a promise of more.

You see an alibi, regardless of what people really think, is just a perception. It's a set of views, observations and assertions that corroborate what you are saying. If enough of those perceptions add weight to circumstantial evidence then black becomes white and night becomes day. And when you're as smart as Liz Langford, well the strings are just there to be pulled. Sean hadn't been pulled for quite a while. That much was obvious.

So what of Liz whilst her husband was out, again, with his friends? Well she was stacking the shelves in Wilkos and straightening the displays and smiling wanly at anyone who passed her, barely recognisable at all as a living, breathing human being – forgettable, dispensable, just as she would have wanted. Just as the most perfect of alibis demanded.

There is sometimes no telling how tenuous is somebody's grip on what is right and what is wrong. You can have charts for this and questionnaires for that, graphs of all sorts of colours, presentations and lectures and doctorates that give you the permission to call yourself a doctor even if you're not even a doctor, a specialist even if you're not a specialist. But what you really need is to be there at the moment when the balance of the scales tips, to witness how small a nudge is required for someone to go from some hope to no hope, to go from clinging on by the fingertips to letting go and taking everyone with them. If you're not there at the precise moment then everything else is just guesswork and coloured pens.

Cracks are appearing all over this nation and not just in the desperate streets of Tottenham or the blazing fires of Croydon. It's everywhere – in the fetid front rooms of the downtrodden, the violent silences of the country kitchen and the frustration of those that try so hard to do what is right. Cracks opening and widening, beckoning and imploring. It's in the eyes of those who stare at the TV though it's not even on and in the two in the morning waking heart-poundings of the debt-ridden and the frantic. And the first thing to go is perspective – especially where love is concerned.

Arguments appear where before there would have been tacit agreement. Flashes of anger turn to outbursts of violence and violence in turn goes from unconscionable to justifiable. It's an insidious movement brought on by external pressures and internal woes, brought on by the fact that forgiveness is seen as a weakness and love as a luxury.

It's straws and backs, that's all. It's messages written by the daughter of a widower found by a woman who is just waiting for the breaking of her heart to feel alive again. Angels or no angels, these are dangerous times that will bring out the very worst in some and the very best in others. Sometimes it takes the prospect of death to jump into your head to make you realise how wonderful is this life.

Little Jon had missed the weekend away with the lads due to work commitments. This was not an unusual occurrence. The Matron in A & E had taken a dislike to him the moment she had met him. She had found him flippant and cocky. He had decided immediately that she must be a lesbian. But boy he knew his stuff. What he lacked in tact he made up for in courage and ability. Where his belief that all women adored him could be called into question, his knowledge of what helped people in a crisis, be it the victim of an accident or a grieving family member, well that could never be debated. He had a natural talent for making people in need feel better and people in power feel worse – an affliction of which he was both aware and proud.

When you're a nurse, wheel-spinning into the hospital car park in silver BMW is a singular pleasure – one of which Little Jon never failed to tire. His car was the suit he never owned and the girlfriend that had always eluded him. It was older than it looked and was practically falling apart within the shiny carcass. From the outside it was stunning. The fact that it passed the MOT each year though was more to do with a dodgy garage in Harold Wood than the efficiency and safety of its composite parts. Little Jon lived on the edge with a glee that fuelled him – whether that edge be saving lives or putting his own life at risk every time he drove to and from work.

So it was that a few days after one of his friends had been hailed a paintballing hero, Ray received a call from Broomfield Hospital to state that one of his other friends had been involved in a serious car accident. Little Jon had come to see his friends as his only true family. Thus, in his barely conscious state, he had given the paramedic Ray's name and number as his next of kin. Fortunately Ray had just got in from work and had not yet started drinking.

On hearing the news about Little Jon and unable to get an answer on Danny's phone, Ray had rammed his car onto the forecourt of The Setting Sun to leave a message with Sean. But Danny was already in there, having been undeniably sick for the day. Rod was with him and both were more than a little squiffy. Despite their condition, they both insisted on joining Ray and leapt into the back of the car.

The AA Routemaster Website states that The Setting Sun, Chelmsford is just over four miles from Broomfield Hospital with an estimated journey time of twelve and a half minutes. Ray made it in six. The windscreen of any car that happened to be behind was battered by cigarette butts that were huzzed out of the windows, front and back by the friends who knew talking wasn't an option - not when one of their own lay in who knows what state, with no-one but them to call on.

Almost instinctively Danny and Rod looked to Ray as the three of them entered the A&E department. A certain shamefulness clung to Rod. He felt as if he hadn't earned the right to be there. He had only known Little Jon for a few weeks after all. And Danny? Well he struggled at the best of times with being confronted with the darker sides of life. It was not a failing. More just something he could not comprehend. But Ray, he had a sense of a duty that took over on such occasions. It didn't mean he was any less terrified, any less emotional. It was just he could force himself to handle the worst. That was all.

"Our mate Jon Heskey was brought in a bit earlier. Car crash. We need to see him," Ray said to the receptionist behind the desk.

"If you'd like to take a seat, I'll be with you in a moment," came the weary reply.

"Look love," said Ray. "Your lot called us down here. We're here. Now tell us where Jon is or we'll just go and find him."

"We have a zero tolerance approach to violence here young man," replied the thoroughly disgruntled receptionist.

"So do I," Ray replied. "We just want to see our mate. We're all his got. At least tell us if he's alive or dead."

The receptionist softened a little, fear turning to compassion. She emitted a tiny sigh and said she would try and find out.

Ray turned to Rod and Danny, mouthed the words 'Let's go,' and strode off through the entrance to the cubicles.

By beautiful chance they happened upon Little Jon almost immediately. He was in the second bay. He had just returned from the x-ray department and had been hooked up to a morphine drip. He was barely recognisable. No description could do it justice. It breaks my heart just to think how close he came to death. It would be over a year before he could walk again. Both legs had been shattered. To this day he believes he got out of that car and walked around the back before collapsing. And you know what? I believe him, shattered legs or not. I believe him and I believe *in* him – in all the good and glorious people in this world. And it will always be so.

"Fuck me," said Danny when he could finally bring himself to move close to his friend who lay in the bed before him, all morphined up and supine.

"No thanks," replied Little Jon, wincing at every word. "Not until you shave." And then he closed his gleaming glazed eyes and drifted off to morphine wonderland, entirely deserving of his rest.

Rod stood on the other side of the curtain, not a part of the scene, adrift from the direct heart of it all. For it was then that light suddenly broke through him, overcoming, overwhelming, subduing and forgiving the dull throbbings that had bubbled in his soul for so long. These were real people, desperate for their mate to be alright for Little Jon was a part of what kept the others going as each of them served the same purpose for one another. Alone this life can be intolerable. Together it can be astonishing. Death isn't where it is mate. It's about love and life and all the pink dolly mixtures you can share. So no longer foster that bitterness - let it out, stand as tall as you can little man and reach for the bang-a-lang stars…

190

24. Prey In The Wilderness

A little silver key is a prize indeed. Whether it be handmade by a perfect beauty sculptor or whether it has fallen from a cheap Christmas cracker. Regardless, there is wonder in a small silver key. And when that key has been forever out of your grasp throughout your whole life and when your whole life has been forever out of your grasp, well, when you have that silvering silver in your hand and your dad is out and that filing cabinet is more or less imploring you to transform its A7 tension into a D chord resolution, there is just one thing you can do. Just move your fingers boy onto those bottom three strings and listen closely to the click lock revolution resolution. Mmmm yeah. Resound and echo and mmmm yeah. Then sigh. And behold.

The top drawer had a piece of paper sellotaped to it with faded writing on it proclaiming the words 'Eastern Region Angel Collective.' The drawers beneath it had similar signs with the names of the the three other regions: the Western Angel Contingent, the North Western Angels, the North Eastern Angel Collective and the Midlands Angel Alliance. Brando turned the key in the lock and pulled open the top drawer, half in awe and half in shame. He knew that if he backed away now he would be backing away forever.

When you spend the latter half of your life retreating, the only place you ever end up is where you started from. And nobody wants to be there. So Brando pulled that drawer open, expecting to find neatly ordered files detailing the various tales, celebrations and exploits of the many angels that hailed from the Essex, Suffolk and Cambridge area.

But what he actually found took his breath away.

There were no files. There were no folders. At first glance it seemed there was nothing in the drawer at all. It was only when Brando put his hand in that he discovered what his eyes had not seen.

He brought forth several sheets of various sized paper and took them over to his father's desk. He remained standing whilst he looked through them. He recognised them immediately as pictures Eryn Rose had created when she was a child – pictures of angels. All the angels, and there were many, were painted and drawn or coloured in with crayon. He remembered then that all Eryn Rose ever created were angels. She would always present them to Renbourne with a big and honest grin accompanied by the words "This one's mummy. And this one too. And this one." And there they were before him – his sister's angels.

It was when Brando spread the pictures out on the desk that he saw one that hadn't been done by Eryn Rose. He recognised it because his little six year old hand had signed it. He had always preferred drawing to painting and colouring – just a black pencil on white paper. It seemed even as a child he had sought clarity – a clarity his adult self had never quite been able to attain. The drawing was of a car with a big engine that stuck out through the bonnet with flames coming from the exhaust. It had huge tires and a round smiley face peering through the windscreen. He had loved cars when he was younger and had dreamed of making the one he had drawn when he grew up so he could give it to his dad.

Holding that flimsy sheet of paper with its crude pencil drawing upon it, well that's when tears came to his eyes. His father had kept it all the years, all these years. How often had he looked at it, admired it, seen that car move, heard it rev, roared with it and smiled with it? All these years. And all at once Brando loved his father with absolute passion. Ah Dad mate. Ah Dad.

The remaining drawers of the filing cabinet were empty, entirely empty. It seemed that even dust particles had left them alone.

Brando put the pictures back in the top drawer and locked the filing cabinet, leaving the key in the lock where it had been prior to his having taken it. He sat down on his father's chair, leaned forward and drew his fingers through his hair, the tips rubbing his scalp back and forth as he gazed at the floor.

So that was the Eastern Region Angel Collective – a notion devised by a grieving husband to perpetuate the dreams of his beautiful wife. And in so doing to bring up a son and a daughter who barely knew her with the idea that their mother had started something wonderful that would change the world. What other way is there to get over losing someone you love? I don't know. I truly don't.

Any ambition to become an angel, to impress his father, to show Eryn Rose he could do it dissipated in the depth of that moment. The pencil car roared and the pencil flames glowed. His dad loved him. His dad was wonderful. And that was enough. He thought of the times his father must have sat just where he was sitting now, looking at the paintings and pictures, staring at the angel rules that were taped to the desk and gazing at the photograph of his wife. There are no words for such moments. None that I have, anyway.

Meanwhile, Liz Langford was on the other side of town waiting for darkness to come and for her husband to return home from 'the hospital.' Really? The hospital? Of course dear. You take your time. The hospital. Liz had plans you see, plans that made so much sense to her. She smiled to herself when Rod had tried to log onto his 'wideawake' document the previous evening, unaware as he was that she had changed the password whilst he was away at The Moon & Sixpence. He'd struggled for a while and given up. Shouldn't have been seeing that angel tart then should he? Rocking back and forth gently on the sofa she felt her life at last had meaning. Ah she was clever was Liz Langford, more clever than anyone had ever given her credit for.

As Rod walked back from Wilkos where Ray had dropped him off so he could buy some cigarettes, he reflected on the turning of his days. It was as if he had gone from watching life on a black and white TV to leaping into a multicolour world of wonder. He wasn't excited as such, for that element of him that once existed had long been subdued to the point where it had lost its spring. And excitement should be bouncy. We all know that. Seeing Little Jon, his jumper scrunched up on the floor of his hospital room, had been the final denouement. He intended to go home and do something he never did – give his wife a hug and tell her he loved her. Cherishing times were ahead for the long haired, leather jacketed man just below midget height. Or so he believed.

When the door clicked and Rod walked in, Jasmine scrambled over the laminated flooring and practically slid into him. Now this was unusual. Rod thought such immediate affection could perhaps be due to the fact that his love of life had been restored and that Jasmine had sensed it. Poor fool. When animals are afraid they will seek help from whoever makes them feel less afraid. For three hours the small, fluffy dog had been contemplating its owner. And as each moment had passed his fear had grown. Animals notice things that we are sometimes slow to see – moods, changes in tension, changes in *in*tention. Jasmine was no different. Still on the poofy side perhaps, but astute nonetheless.

Liz looked up at Rod as he approached. She was still seated on the sofa when he sat down beside her. She allowed him to put his arm across the back of her shoulders (as far as he could reach anyway) and she took her eyes momentarily away from the television when he told her that he loved her. Jasmine looked on from a distance, shaking imperceptibly.

"So do you want to do anything tonight then? Go out or something?" asked Rod, his mind clearer now than it had been for so long.

But all Liz heard were the guilty words of a faithless man. Each syllable turned to dust the moment it entered her ear, not even giving her mind a chance to appraise the question being asked.

"Liz," Rod persevered. "Are you ok? I was just asking if you wanted to go out tonight. For dinner or something. We never do that."

This time she deigned to answer.

"To the pub I suppose?" She turned to him as she spoke, let him feel the force of her countenance and then once more looked away.

194

"Anywhere you want. Entirely up to you."

"Anywhere?"

"Anywhere."

"With you?"

"Yes. Both of us. Anywhere. Whatever you want."

Liz stood up and turned to face her husband. She was thoroughly enjoying herself and the look on Rod's face, that confused, stupid, idiotic look just added to her joy. From his point of view, sitting there, looking up at his wife, there seemed to be so much more than an inch in height between them now.

"I have to pop out for a while," said Liz. "What time is it now?"

"About six I think."

"I'll only be half an hour."

"So we'll go somewhere when you get back, get something to eat?" said Rod, leaning forward, feeling at last that he was getting somewhere.

"Of course," said Liz. "Anything you want."

Rod felt a sense of relief. It would be just like old times, he and Liz taking a stroll down Moulsham Street, maybe get a curry or something. Good stuff.

Jasmine stayed under the table for a few more minutes after Liz had left the flat, emerging only when the smell of perfume had finally dispersed.

Sean was standing behind the bar when Liz pushed open the door and entered The Setting Sun. It was not unusual for him to be the only person in the pub, not unusual at all. Most of the time he preferred it that way. Not a great business model it has to be said.

"Liz. What a nice surprise. What can I get you?"

If any of the lads had been around to listen to Sean ask that question they may well have ended up getting barred. He sounded like a bad actor who, despite only having one line, had still managed to fail in delivering it with sincerity. The irony was that he really meant what he said.

"I guess I could have a quick drink," replied Liz in as sultry a voice as she could manage.

"So you've got time for a quickie?" asked Sean leaning towards her.

Goodness me.

"You are funny, Sean. I'll just have a coke please."

"Coming up."

Stop it…

Sean poured himself a pint of lager after he had handed Liz her drink.

"This one's on me," he said, nodding in a self-congratulatory fashion, as if he'd just bought her a boat or something.

Liz smiled and stood at the bar, sipping her coke. Sean gulped on his lager. It was as if the sounds of her sipping and his gulping met somewhere in the air above the bar, intertwining, forming a base union, a sloppy kiss, atom upon atom.

"There is one thing you can do for me actually, Sean."

"Ask away."

"Well it's for Rod, if I'm honest."

The shine went from Sean's eyes in an instant. His mouth, exhausted at the effort it had taken to hold a smile for so long, reverted back in relief to form a more comfortable sneer.

Men, thought Liz, *they lust after you, cheat on you or reject you. Sean, Rod, Brando. Lust, cheat, reject.*

"Go on."

"It's just he's got it into his head that he wants to cook something for dinner, some beef thing, but he needs a sharp knife to cut it with. I don't know what he's playing at really. I can't remember the last time he cooked and he's never done anything other than hook stuff out of a can or put it in a microwave. He was very insistent though. About the knife."

"I'll see what I can find," muttered Sean.

"Oh don't be like that," said Liz, reaching over and touching his hand. "You'd be doing me a favour too. You really would."

And as easily as that the sneer was roused from its ragged bed to once more become a smile. Minutes later Liz Langford was walking back to the flat in Pearce Manor with a very sharp eight-inch knife wrapped in a stained tea-towel. Rod was at that moment splashing on perhaps a little too much aftershave whilst Sean contented himself with licking the lipstick from the edge of Liz's empty glass.

Moulsham Street leads from Trinity Park down to the dual carriageway that feeds off the Army and Navy Roundabout and skirts the town centre, running parallel with New London Road. Whereas its companion is sparse in its offerings, the bottom end of Moulsham Street has everything a man might need when going out with his wife. You've got cafés, restaurants, take-aways, cashpoints and pubs. There's even a gay bar, a sex shop and, if it all goes wrong, a florist. It's not Covent Garden but, for Rod and Liz, Moulsham Street had always made them feel that they were stepping out into the bright lights of the big city.

Though Rod and Liz walked hand in hand towards the end of Moulsham Street, barely a word was uttered by either of them. Rod took this as a sign that they were comfortable in each others company. Little did he know that his wife just wanted to get this part of the evening over with as quickly as she could. Her thoughts were elsewhere. Lust could wait, but cheat and rejection, well she couldn't help but breathe a little harder when she thought of what was to come.

"Small doner, mate," said Rod to Mr Ram, co-owner of the late night culinary paradise that is Mr Ram and Mrs Cod's take-away/eat-in establishment.

"Chili sauce?"

"Yep."

"Salad?"

"Not much."

"Eat in or take away?"

"Eat in. Cheers."

"Anything else?"

"The wife wants sausage in batter and chips."

"Eat in or take away?"

"Well, eat in. We're out for dinner."

Rod looked quizzically at Mr Ram who looked equally quizzically back at Rod.

"Ten pounds seventy. Salt, vinegar and sauce is on the tables."

"Cheers mate."

Liz watched Rod as he carried their food over to where she sat at a table in the back corner. He was smiling broadly as if he had just snared his prey in the wilderness and cooked it over an open fire to present to his cavewoman wife.

As they faced each other across the small table, Liz with her back to the wall and Rod with his back to everybody, people came in, queued and left, wandering back out into the evening, food in a bag, and a wonderful sense of satisfaction in their hearts. Some would eat as they walked, others would hurry their steps, the heat of their meal burning through the increasingly soggy wrapping urging them on to their homes. And when they get there some will sit in front of the television eating from the bag on their lap whilst others may warm a plate and sit at a table, their meal beautifully presented and eaten with decorum. Ah Mr Ram and Mrs Cod – purveyors of sustenance for the needy of Chelmsford!

Rod worked his way through his kebab, manfully holding back the chilli tears and eating the salad with a grudging acceptance that at least he was getting some healthy nourishment. Liz ate mechanically, barely observing her plate as she did so. She forever looked over Rod's bowed head, her hand dropping to pluck chips like one of those electrical grabbing machines in the arcades. She made sure to save her sausage in batter until Rod had finished eating. He looked at her adoringly as she slowly munched her way through it, mayonnaise dripping from her bottom lip. He was in complete ecstasy – she was in complete control.

Once back in the flat, at just gone 11 pm, Rod and Liz went to bed. Rod fell asleep almost immediately. The moment she heard her husband snore, Liz's eyes flashed open. She crept from the bed, slipped into her jeans and put a t-shirt on. She removed the tea-towel containing the knife from the bottom drawer of the cabinet beside her bed and went into the lounge, placing it on the table. Having checked that the password on the computer was still the same as she had changed it to, Liz picked up Rod's leather jacket from the sofa and put it on. Finally, she took the knife from the tea-towel and secreted it carefully in the inside pocket of the jacket. Thus dressed and equipped she entered the night.

The moon gazed down for a moment before drawing a veil of clouds across its vision. It was Friday 26th August 2012 and not a star could be seen in the black Chelmsford sky as Liz Langford strode purposefully towards the house of angels.

25. Smile Wide Across My Forever Skies

Brando was sitting on his bed when he got the call. Until that point he had managed to retain the feeling of belonging that had been induced following his opening of the filing cabinet in his father's room. Somehow his heart beat slower and his thoughts had a less abrasive feel to them. All that harmony though was shaken up when his mobile phone vibrated and Liz Langford made her proposal.

"Why would Rod want to meet with me?" Brando asked. "It's not like I've ever met him before."

"I don't know," replied Liz from the payphone just outside Trinity Park. "He just does. He says it's important."

"Where?"

"The park. Where you took me that first time. On that bench."

"What time?"

"Half past eleven."

"Can't this wait until tomorrow? It's really late."

"No."

"Can I not just speak to him? Is he there?"

"He just left."

"Oh, ok."

There was a pause.

"Aren't you even going to ask me how I am?" Liz asked, doing her best to make her voice sound as sexy as she could.

"Sorry. How are you?"

"Do you even care?" she replied, her voice all lead now, bristling.

"But you asked me to ask you."

"My point is I shouldn't have to, not after what we had."

"But we didn't have anything," said Brando, becoming more and more confused, the short-lived sense of peace he had so recently enjoyed oozing from him.

"Time for you to go," Liz stated, plain and clear. "Time for you to go."

She hung up the phone leaving Brando to shake his head, take a deep breath and sigh. Helping people shouldn't always be easy, he thought, as he pulled on his shoes and left the quiet house.

Renbourne had arrived home half an hour or so earlier and was shut up in his study. Though he heard the front door close, he made no move to see whether it was Brando or Eryn Rose who had left, for his mind was on other things.

Eryn Rose however did hear the door close. Having spoken to Brando briefly earlier in the evening she had sensed a change in him. He had seemed more like the boy he used to be prior to adulthood and all its complications being thrust upon him. He had actually been a pleasure to be around. Still, she worried about him. When she had heard him going down the stairs and out of the house, she knew the only right thing for a sister and angel to do was to follow him and make sure he was not getting himself into trouble.

But when Eryn Rose reached the darkness of the sparsely lit street she had no idea in which direction Brando had gone. Angels may be archetypes but even they like their mobile phones.

"Brando?"

Brando fully expected the call to once more be from Liz, perhaps checking if he had yet left to meet Rod; or perhaps the call was from Rod this time, chiding him for not already being at their agreed destination. He was relieved to hear his sister's voice.

"Hi Eryn Rose? You okay?"

"Are *you* okay? Where are you going? I heard you leave the house. It's really late you know."

"Your man Rod wants to meet me. Seemed important. I didn't want to disturb you."

"I'll come with you. Where are you meeting him?"

"Trinity Park. The bench by the swings and slides. Don't worry though. I'll be fine. Go back to bed. Dad will worry."

"I've left now anyway. See you soon!"

"Okay. See you."

Brando had just climbed over the gates to the park when Eryn Rose had called and he was already through the car park by the time their conversation was at an end. He wondered how Rod was going to get into the park. He doubted he would be able to climb the gate. He knew Eryn Rose would manage it but worried a little about her bare feet on the rusty metal.

The moon was full on this late August night and Trinity Park was all space and silence and shadows. The air was still and the grass was cold and spiky. Less than a mile away, in town, alcohol was spilling out into the street, people were falling over one another and beating hearts were breaking. Sirens were ever on the verge of wailing and so many people were never going to do this to themselves again. Chips fell from shoulders to the pavement and taxis lay in stately wait, ready to receive the debris of an Essex Friday night.

Come gather round people wherever you roam
and admit that the future around you has grown...

Liz had been waiting in the trees behind the bench where she had told Brando they would meet. She was low down, her ears alert for the slightest sound. She crouched on the balls of her feet and she pressed the palms of her hands into the dirt for balance. It seemed all she was missing was a tail. The birds above regarded her with apprehension and the branches shook a little yet there was no wind, not even a breeze.

Brando walked towards the bench with a slight smile upon his face, a smile of peace, issuing forth from a feeling that he was not only doing good work but that the basis from which he was doing that work was solid indeed. He saw now what it was to be selfless. He did not, however, see Liz Langford hiding in the trees just a yard behind the bench upon which he now sat.

Back in The Setting Sun, Sean was ready to close up. Ray, Danny and Alex had been in for the last couple of hours. They'd had a good laugh and managed to cheer themselves up after the strictures of the hospital where they'd been with Little Jon. They had ended up being ushered out by the night staff on the ward as visiting time was over and they were being just a bit *too* loud.

"You all need to get going now," said Sean. "Come on. On your way."

Danny downed the remainder of his pint in the hope of securing another one but a shake of the landlord's miserable head put an end to that plan.

"Come on lads," said Ray. "We can catch the burger van if we go now."

"Cheers, Sean," said Alex, closing the door behind him.

Sean came out from behind the bar and bolted the door.

"Who hasn't got a knife to cut up a piece of meat?" he muttered to himself. "Fucking midget," he added as he turned off the lights and stomped up the stairs. "Doesn't know how lucky he is."

The sight of a tranquil park before him and an empty playground to his right confirmed to Brando that he had perhaps just been moving too fast all these years. Now, when everything was still, he had a chance of understanding. The car in the picture he had painted as a child for his father, that hadn't moved in all these years. What had changed though, what had kept moving out of control was his view of himself and those around him. But when the swing no longer swings and the slide no longer slides there is a time for stillness and for perspective.

Such thoughts were Brando Anderson thinking when the knife went in.

Initially he only felt a slight pain as it pierced the skin of his abdomen. It was the shock that was worse, almost electric in its power and its suddenness. This was swiftly followed by a coldness that spread through his lower body, emanating from the blade of the knife that was now inches inside him. Just as his body was becoming attuned to what was happening, Liz withdrew the knife and that was when Brando experienced the most intense, the most violent, the most shattering pain he had ever experienced in his life. His whole body felt it. He began to panic and this just made things worse. He slid from the bench, his legs outstretched and the back of his head against the wooden frame. Just as the panic exploded into his mind, the coldness in his abdomen began to feel warm as blood rushed to the stricken area. Rather than be the re-enforcements he so badly needed, the blood bled straight on through onto his t-shirt, onto the grass, onto the earth and into the shadows. Not one coherent thought entered his mind during those final moments. Just before he passed out, the pain had almost completely subsided, yet he had not sufficient breath within his lungs even to manage a sigh of relief.

As Eryn Rose was climbing over the large iron gate into Trinity Park so Liz Langford was sneaking through a gap in the hedge just a hundred yards to her left. And as Eryn's bare feet touched the dewy grass so Liz stepped onto the unforgiving pavement. By the time Liz was safely back in the flat where her husband lay sleeping, Eryn Rose was staring at the still figure slumped on the ground before her.

Oh God, too late you realise you're standing in your brother's blood. The soles of your feet so used to the cool give of this wondrous land are now warm and squelched with the deep dark red of a life drained, a life that has just slipped away. There is nothing to shatter and nothing to splinter. A scream is just a breath, a gasp. And what can you do but stare? Nothing has prepared you for this. Brando's eyes are open wide yet it is not Brando that looks through them. His soul has fled relieved. His heart has stopped beating like the final beat of a symphony. It's over. Yet it has just begun. Ah angel float above it all now, above the dark grass and the standstill and the trees and the town and the city and this earth.

Go, go, go and smile wide across my forever skies whilst your body is limp and your blood clots.

Eryn Rose just stood there for a while. Then she sat on the ground, her bare legs crossed. She looked up and carried on looking up until her neck ached. She was looking for her mother amongst the stars, searching for some sign that would tell her what to do. But none came. So she phoned the police – and they came instead.

Brando Anderson was pronounced dead on arrival at Broomfield Hospital. Pronounced and noted and signed and counter-signed, a life gone from this temporary earth.

It was gone four o'clock in the morning before Eryn Rose and Renbourne returned back home. The birds were chirping, causing the dawn to break, and the sun spread itself lazily across the horizon in order to consume the maudlin moon. Sometimes the moon just sees too much.

The study in the house of angels was quiet as ever it was. Throughout the previous evening Renbourne had known that a change was coming. For when he had opened the top drawer of the filing cabinet to look at his children's pictures, Brando's car was on the top. The engine itself may have revved so shocked was the man who had gazed then upon it. It was then that he knew the Eastern Region Angel Collective was no more. He was a widower. His daughter was a cleaner and his son unemployed. That was the Eastern Region Angel Collective. The dreams he had dreamed, the words he had weaved and the awe he had instilled in Eryn Rose and Brando, well, as far as he was concerned, all was over.

They say there is a process for grief. They say that it starts with denial, followed by guilt and anger and loneliness before adjustment, reconstruction and hope pull you through. When Renbourne had lost his wife, angel that she was, he had somehow started at the end of this process. He had begun with hope, a hope that was bestowed upon him by the woman he loved. You can't deny death but you can bring hope. And that is what Renbourne had tried to do. It was all he had been able to do. All those other steps were for people that didn't believe in angels. But what to do now, now that Brando too was gone?

Renbourne was in his chair. Eryn Rose was sitting on the floor, her back to the door, her eyes red raw and redundant.

"Eryn Rose?"

She looked up and met her father's tired eyes.

"Yes, dad?"

"I love you."

And all Eryn Rose could do was cry.

"I love you, Eryn Rose. I love you."

Rod Langford awoke that Saturday morning with his little arm across his wife's shoulders. He breathed deep and satisfied. Oftentimes, in the old days, the chirping of the birds would irritate him to the extent he would cram a pillow over his head whilst swearing and writhing. But these days things were different. FRUGALITY was having an effect and he had good friends. He was seeing with new eyes now. Even Jasmine the poofy dog seemed slightly less, well, poofy than he had previously been. These observations came to him as he lay there in a beautiful doze.

What Rod didn't know though was that his wife hadn't slept all night. She had been absolutely buzzing from the moment she had discarded the knife, fingerprints wiped and all wrapped up in Rod's leather jacket – thrown into the trees where she had been hiding. Buzzing, revving, however you want to describe it. She had never felt like this before. It was the thrill of finally having an impact, of crawling out from beneath the shade that had ever been upon her. What would the day bring? And the following day? And the one after that? They would give her a name, she thought, one day, when it all came out. What would they call her? Clever for sure. Psychopath? Maybe. She wasn't keen on psychopath though. Far too dreary, too commonplace. Perhaps it would be better if nobody ever knew? In that way she would be even more powerful than she already felt. The choice was hers alone to make.

Wide-awake.

26. The Heart Of My Beat

It was just after half past ten in the morning when the Police knocked on Rod's door. Eryn Rose had informed them at the scene of the murder that Brando had been going to meet him. Rod's jacket and the knife had been recovered almost immediately with Eryn Rose confirming the distinctive jacket to be Rod's. Shock had overwhelmed her soon after and it was only following a fitful red-eye sleep that she had been able to remember Rod's surname and where he lived. The records in the Eastern Region Angel Collective drawer had not been of much use.

Liz had gone outside the flat shortly after nine to walk Jasmine. During this time she had called the Police 'concerned' about a document she had found on her husband's computer. She said she was now out of the flat as she felt worried about what he may be capable of. When Eryn Rose's call came through an hour or so afterwards confirming Rod's surname and address, it was enough for the Police to come knocking. And whilst all this was happening, Rod had dozed back to sleep, only to be awoken by a banging on his front door.

You know sometimes how you get a sense that all is not right, some primeval prodding deep down inside you as old as time? Well that's what Rod experienced even after the, admittedly hefty, first knock on his door. He knew immediately that his life was about to be thrown completely out of control. He could also sense that he was very much alone. At the third knock, once he had pulled on an old Def Leppard t-shirt, he opened the door and just let it all happen.

Rod went with the Police officers and sat in the back of the Police Car, an officer either side of him. Two other policemen, he saw now, were speaking to Liz who held Jasmine's lead with one hand whilst she wrote something on a piece of paper with the other. Rod wasn't aware then that she was giving the officers the password to the computer in the flat. He thought, as the two officers approached the car, that he saw Liz crying. She certainly appeared to be shaking, anyway, her shoulders moving up and down causing the dog lead to tense intermittently. Rod tried to turn to look at her as the car pulled away but he couldn't quite see over the back seat due to his littleness.

Living in the opposite block of flats, Danny had been staring out the window when he saw the Police car arrive. When he had seen Rod being led towards it he had hurriedly pulled on some jeans and stumbled down the three flights of stairs, stubbing a toe as he did so. By the time he emerged into the light, the Police car had gone. Cursing his toe injury and considering the possibility that it could lead to a blood clot, he hobbled over to where Liz was just letting herself back into the block of flats.

"What the fuck's going on?" He asked. "What are they doing taking Rod away?"

When Liz turned around she had managed, in just a few seconds, to contort her face into the very picture of a distraught wife. She had even been able to squeeze out a tear.

"You don't know him like I do. You don't," she whimpered. "You don't know him like you think you do."

At that, she turned, walked into the block of flats and left Danny standing outside entirely bemused. He felt a little sick and was unsure whether it was due to the shock of seeing his friend carted away in the back of a Police car or if indeed a clot was forming in his toe that would swiftly make its way to his heart and kill him stone dead. Either way, he decided he had to phone Ray.

By the time Danny, Ray and Alex had convened at The Setting Sun, Sean had already, rather gleefully it must be said, put two and two together. News of Brando's murder had been on BBC Essex Radio since mid-morning and by lunchtime when he opened the doors of the pub Liz had already called him to say that his knife was missing

209

from the drawer in the kitchen and that the Police had come for Rod. Ray had gone for his morning run and had seen that the entrance to Trinity Park had been taped off by the Police. Alex had, like Sean, heard of the murder on the radio and Danny of course had seen Rod taken away, yet none of them could believe that Rod would have had anything to do with the killing.

"Three lagers," said Ray. The smile on Sean's face irked him.

"All happening today isn't it?" remarked Sean as he poured the drinks.

Ray ignored him. Danny and Alex had gone out the back to have a cigarette.

"I said it's all happening today isn't?"

"I heard you the first time. How much is that?"

"Same as it always is. Nine pounds thirty."

Ray paid and took two of the pints out to the beer garden before coming back for his own.

"You hear about the murder over the way, Ray? Terrible thing. Really terrible. In Chelmsford of all places."

"Yeah. I heard," replied Ray taking a large gulp of his pint.

"Rumour has it they got someone for it already. So they say," continued Sean. "Local lad by all accounts."

Ray looked Sean straight in the eye and managed by his well-practiced look of intimidation to at least lessen some of the glee in the landlord's eyes before going back out to join his friends.

The three lads sat on one of the benches and smoked in silence. They were half way through their pints before any of them spoke.

"You really think they've picked Rod up for killing that bloke?" asked Alex. He actually wondered if he had even asked the question for all that followed was more silence.

Ray took a deep breath, bit his bottom lip and lit another cigarette.

"My fucking toe's killing me," said Danny.

And even through the closed rear door of the pub they could all clearly hear the high pitched whistle of a man who welcomes the misery of others as much as most of us welcome a peaceful night's sleep.

It was the following day before the Police were able to secure a search warrant for the flat. They took the computer and the angel session letters that Eryn Rose had written to Rod. Liz had left them on the sofa so they could not be missed. Rod appeared at Chelmsford Magistrates Court on the Monday morning and was remanded in custody to HMP Chelmsford with the case being referred to the Crown Court at a date to be arranged. And from the moment of his arrest the only words he spoke were to the Magistrate to confirm his name, his court name – Roderick Stephen Giles Langford.

Although he was remanded to HMP Chelmsford, he wasn't there, not really. For in his mind, a mind that had been touched by friendship and belonging, he was somewhere else entirely…

Rod sees not four walls and a metal door but Highlands Park, Chelmsford – the venue for the annual V music festival and the glorious English grounds of Highlands House. He sees it so well because he is sitting astride a branch in the tallest tree you ever saw. He is like the cabin-boy on the main topmast of a pirate ship, scouring the green grass seas for wonderment and adventure. And below him at the base of the trunk are his crew – Ray, Danny, Alex and Little Jon. They are swigging from bottles of cheap wine, their backs to the tree and their eyes closed in blissful bliss. Ah this ship sails and this ship will never come in!

But then there is a sound far off. Rod the cabin-boy is the first to be hear it. He peers into the distance and smudges on the horizon turn swiftly into moving human forms, no, running human forms! The sound is a wail and the wail is a siren and the human forms are the Police. They flood the horizon and wade up the hill towards the tree, scuffing their shiny black boots on the deep dark earth, stamping the grass down, thumping their way towards the tree and towards Rod.

And that's when another sound rears up. No, not a sound, something much more powerful, men together, men singing a song that swells and breaks and shimmers through the beauty of all that is right in this world. As Rod looks down he sees the lads have discarded their bottles. Yes, they have put down their bottles. More than that they stand in a line, their arms across one another's shoulders and they are belting out Jerusalem by William Blake my hero, my all-time hero, with all the power any man could possess.

And did those feet in ancient time.
Walk upon England's mountains green:
And was the holy Lamb of God,
On England's pleasant pastures seen!

The Police breach the top of the hill. There are hundreds of them all in step, all rigid and unbending, tramping and unyielding, imbalanced in their desire for their bird of prey.

And did the Countenance Divine,
Shine forth upon our clouded hills?
And was Jerusalem builded here,
Among these dark Satanic Mills?

As the Police do rise upon the crest of the hill so does the sun take its place on the skyline, casting into shadow those that would be cast into shadow and lighting in blaze and fury those who are friends of mine. Ah lads. Ah lads! You sing so sweet and you are the very beat of my heart, the heart of my beat!

Bring me my Bow of burning gold;
Bring me my Arrows of desire:
Bring me my Spear: O clouds unfold!

And Rod, he gazes now not down or across but up towards the skies that the whole world sees. He wants of nothing and he desires nothing. For what he has truly come to know is that he is a good man. His friends below sing still, oh how they sing and with every note so he is fulfilled. I am a good man. I am a good man.

I will not cease from Mental Fight,
Nor shall my Sword sleep in my hand:
Till we have built Jerusalem,
In England's green & pleasant Land

Before long the tree is surrounded and the lads take once more to their bottles of cheap wine. Their song is sung and the world hears. It does. I promise. But it's a big old tree, the tallest in the land and Rod is at the very top of it now looking for all the world as if he is about to cast himself off into the great wide open.

Rod Langford was never born and he will never die. He is an angel, an idea, a thought, a spasm, a lightening, a moment. He bursts and he shimmers and he retires and he wavers. An angel is an angel only. The sands shift. Volcanoes rumble. Even the seas sigh. Rod Langford is the mellow in the honey, the cool in the deep hot blue, the breaking of the wave and the shimmering soft of high, high comfort. He is the sparkle and the glint, the hint of a hint of a hint. He is rapture and he is fantastical. Where others wander, he soars and where you dream he inspires and cracks and breaks into a million different suns that will just shower and float into the ether of all your wondabulous thinkings.

And can he fly?
Can he fly?
You better believe it.

213

Summer stuttered to an end and the shrouded brown months of autumn eventually unveiled another stark winter. Christmas came and went. But there would be no chancers delivering poor quality spirits to The Setting Sun on New Years Day 2012. For Sean Parsons was in Almeria, a town in the Andalusian Province of Southern Spain. It was a region in which Sergio Leone had shot his westerns and John Lennon had reportedly written Strawberry Fields Forever. Clearly it was a place for outlaws if ever there was one.

"What a difference a year makes," said Sean, sipping on a glass of red wine as the warm mid-day breeze sought to lure people into their golden siesta slumbers.

After much delay, Sean had at last received the proceeds of his mother's will. He had almost immediately given notice on the lease at The Setting Sun and had begun to make regular trips to Almeria to look for the bar of his dreams.

Liz Langford took her eyes off the small white building opposite where they both sat. She looked at Sean across the small café table and sipped some wine of her own.

"You've got egg on your shirt," she said.

"No I haven't. Anyway, there's plenty more from now on where that came from."

"The egg?"

"No. The shirt. God. And when I get that place over there up and running it will be like the rest of our lives never happened."

The notion of 'a clean slate' appealed to Liz. She had visited Rod just once during the intervening period. The trial date, at which she would be giving evidence for the prosecution, was set for February. She thought about it only fleetingly, much as you or I may occasionally call to mind a concert or a show for which we bought tickets some months before the event. Any initial excitement has waned leaving in its place an acknowledgement that at least you know what you are doing on that particular day.

The evidence against Rod was extensive – the distinctive jacket at the scene, the lack of an alibi, the fingerprints on poor Brando's calling card, whisperings in the pub that his wife was having an affair and of course the 'wideawake' document that had been transformed from the ramblings of a sad man into a confession. The fact that Rod had barely spoken a word to anyone, other than those mates of his that visited all the time, even the one who could hardly walk, well Liz did not consider that he was doing himself many favours.

Liz looked back again at the plain white building, pushed herself back from the table and walked across the road to stand outside it, wishing she could just lock herself within its walls and never have to breathe one single breath outside them. Sean, meanwhile, took the opportunity to lean over and lick the lipstick from the edge of her wine glass.

Epilogue

There is a type of albatross called The Wandering Albatross. It lives on the oceans of the southern hemisphere and can spend months and months in the air without ever needing to touch the earth. It lives for up to eighty years and can weigh as much as two stone. The Light-Mantled Albatross can dive nearly thirteen metres into the ocean. That is *into* the ocean. Thirteen metres deep on down.

And the albatross, well it dances – my god does it dance! It preens and it points and it calls and it stares and it clacks and it absolutely hootly dootly bedazzles this entire world. Yet who of us can say we have seen it? Who of us has witnessed this bird that nobody sees?

Whilst in the air the albatross is the wonder of all wonderments, yet on land it is but a clumsy fool, stiggering and staggering and tripping over its own befuddled feet. In the air it just catches the wailing Donovan wind and it is the sweet troubled fingers of Peter Green. It soars and it cor, cor, cors and it whispers to the heavens from the depths of its beatings – it is magnificent. Oh it is.

But it doesn't stop there. For what's the point of being so incredible if you don't change the world?

The bird that nobody sees. The bird that nobody sees. The albatross is the embodiment only, the symbol, the picture, the badge on the lapel, the fading twinkle of the jingle jangle tambourine. But there are deeper meanings to all things, flittings and floatings that come from within, not without. Flittings and floatings. Angels, my friend. Angels.

An angel is not some sentient being suspended above a stable or crushed upon the wall of a church all harsh and static and unmoving. We are all angels, it's just sometimes we don't realise it. But once we do, well, we will float and we will catch the Donovan wind and we will dive into the oceans of this world and we will soar into its heavens – even though the streets of those heavens are lined with pubs and schools and rambledown houses and toppermost heights of concrete and steeples.

And we will not just waft over the southern oceans and stigger-stagger upon the land. We will float and we will dance into the very lives of all those that need us – we will bring hope to this nation. From the second we awake we will bring hope.

Come all ye.
Come all ye.

Come catch the fine breeze with me…

Printed in Great Britain
by Amazon.co.uk, Ltd.,
Marston Gate.